W9-AYF-234

Loving
Leah

OTHER COVENANT BOOKS AND AUDIO BOOKS BY
LYNNE LARSON:

In the Shadow of an Angel

Saving Lucie Cole

Another Time for Love

Loving Leah

★A NOVEL★

Lynne Larson

Covenant Communications, Inc.

Cover images: *Beautiful Woman in Historical Dress* © eaniton, courtesy veer.com, *Defending Fort Fisher* © HultonArchive, courtesy istockphoto.com, *Confederate Flag in Grunge* © kaarsten, courtesy istockphoto.com

Cover design copyright © 2016 by Covenant Communications, Inc.

Published by Covenant Communications, Inc.
American Fork, Utah

Copyright © 2016 by Lynne Larson
All rights reserved. No part of this book may be reproduced in any format or in any medium without the written permission of the publisher, Covenant Communications, Inc., P.O. Box 416, American Fork, UT 84003. The views expressed within this work are the sole responsibility of the author and do not necessarily reflect the position of Covenant Communications, Inc., or any other entity.

This is a work of fiction. The characters, names, incidents, places, and dialogue are either products of the author's imagination, and are not to be construed as real, or are used fictitiously.

Printed in the United States of America
First Printing: April 2016

21 20 19 18 17 16   10 9 8 7 6 5 4 3 2 1

ISBN 978-1-68047-168-7

For Kent

Acknowledgments

THOSE WHO TAKE UPON THEMSELVES the task of writing historical novels owe a great deal to the people who actually lived through the event or time period being remembered. Their actions, villainous or heroic, make the story worth creating and ultimately worth reading. In the case of this book, which recounts a tragic wartime massacre carried out against civilians, a debt is also owed the dead. While many of these very real victims are seen only in the background of this narrative, their innocent suffering should never be forgotten.

Additionally, I'm grateful to the staff at Covenant Communications, particularly my superb editor, Stacey Turner, for recognizing the intrinsic value of historical fiction, for nurturing this novel toward publication, and for loving Leah enough to let me tell her story.

Part
One

A Mormon Girl

Chapter One

★ ★ ★ ★ ★ ★ ★ ★ ★ ★ ★ ★ ★ ★

I FELL IN LOVE FOR the first time when I was fourteen years old and had the sense of a sparrow. Leah Donaldson was eighteen, I believe, and the most beautiful creature I had ever seen. She viewed me as a child, of course, and had no notion of my obsession. But my world changed when she became a part of it, and life would never be as it once was.

She came to work for us the winter of 1863, late in the season when the icy winds whistling across our Kansas prairie brought more than frostbite and bitterness with them. Leah's lovely presence stood in contrast to the leaden skies and the haunting fear that the war, stalled by cold and snow, would soon visit us again. There were no major engagements in Kansas during the Rebellion—no Gettysburgs or Antietams or Bull Runs. But our eastern counties braced themselves each spring for something more insidious— vigilantes, or Bushwhackers as we called them, led by men like William Clarke Quantrill, George Todd, or Bloody Bill Anderson, raiders from Missouri who wrapped themselves in the Confederate flag but were no more than brutal murderers preying upon the innocent. Leah, new to our county and coming from Iowa as she did, couldn't have guessed how specific the threats would be or the price she would pay because of them. She was a Mormon girl on her way to Zion. Her time with us was meant to be merely a stopping place along the road. Little did any of us know how fate would change those expectations.

"I've found a young woman to keep the house and see to your lessons while I'm away," my father told us, and that was the first we heard of what a Mormon was.

We lived on the edge of Lawrence in a fine Victorian house that befit my father's title, State Senator Stephen Pace, and we might have spent our days in pleasant contentment—every summer watching the waves of Kansas wheat turn golden and feeling the vast blue skies draw us close to heaven—were it not for the troubled times that plagued us. Long before the war, political division and hatred over slavery bled Kansas of its innocence. The war only brought further bitterness as families sent their sons to battle and became sworn enemies of former friends who had chosen the other side. Such issues haunted all the border states, but they were particularly acute in Kansas, where crusaders like John Brown had already stirred up a hornet's nest of local animosity.

My father's politics and abolitionist convictions were well-known, and we were used to enduring partisan bickering if not occasional violence. But there was more trouble in the wind for us than just hatred over states' rights and slavery.

My mother's death, coming quite suddenly and unexpectedly, turned our home into a solemn, mournful place and made the war, as bad as it was, almost an afterthought. She died at harvest time from an outbreak of typhoid that also took some of our neighbors. Mother struggled against the illness, I remember, reluctant to leave us, but she finally drifted off, knowing that my sister, Addie, was recovering from the same affliction.

My father came home for the funeral considerably shaken and left again almost immediately to rejoin the Kansas Fourteenth Regiment of the Union army. The war, then in its first year, seemed to be a welcome distraction, and we rarely saw him in the months that followed. He wrote letters and occasionally sent souvenirs—bullet fragments, a captured Rebel flag, an insignia patch—but he seemed to prefer the clamor of the battlefield to the silence and sadness of a house that had "lost its soul," as our housekeeper, Mrs. Kreiger, said. It was true. My mother's conspicuous absence cast a shadow over everything—until Leah Donaldson was literally dropped on our front porch.

The day before she came, my father sat with Addie and me in the parlor and announced the new arrangement, which had come about suddenly during one of his rare visits home. He was a broad-shouldered man, my father. That day, his long legs were bent and spread apart as he leaned forward in his chair, a hand on each knee, his heavy boots flat on the carpet. "The war necessitates me being gone a great deal of the time," he began solemnly, directing his words mainly toward me, "and Addie is of an age to require a woman's gentleness. Mrs. Kreiger has done her part, but she's too old to keep up with Addie. I believe the girl I've found will do that to my satisfaction and perhaps teach you a thing or two as well, Ethan." He paused, searching for something else to say, unaccustomed to domestic issues. "She's well trained—a Mormon girl, I'm told, lost from her people when the bulk of them were driven out west in the forties. Amos Willard brought her down from Iowa to be a nursemaid to his wife, but Sarah Willard wouldn't have a Mormon in her house. 'Those people have strange ways,' she said, so Willard has been looking to find the girl another situation."

"What's a Mormon?" I asked, wondering why my father would accept a strange woman that Sarah Willard had refused. My mother's death had left an emptiness; now a stranger was coming to make up for the loss, as far as that was possible, and she was already a refugee from someone else's kitchen.

"The Mormons are a religious sect that's been beaten about from pillar to post because they're different," my father answered simply. "But I've got nothing against them. This girl, Leah Donaldson, has certainly done no harm, and you're to treat her with respect no matter how she worships."

"Why does Mrs. Willard think she's strange?"

"Sarah Willard is a fool, and there are plenty like her. See that you're not one of them, Ethan. Heaven holds no place for bigots."

I glanced quickly at Addie, who was peering wide-eyed at our father, confused by his bluntness. She was four years old, seldom spoke, and though oblivious to the meaning of most things, fully sensitive to tones. Her honey-colored hair and blue eyes made her almost cherubic, and her ever-present dimples always melted hearts.

Noting her bewilderment and with an effort at gentleness, Pa bent and touched her cheek. "You're not to worry, Addie. Papa will leave you in good hands." Then he turned back to me with sterner words. "Could be this Mormon girl has more brains than Sarah Willard ever did. You let her teach you what she knows."

"Yes, sir. I will."

"They're Christian folk, these Mormons," he continued briskly. "Nothing Leah Donaldson says is gonna hurt you. I've seen the girl. I've talked to her. The only thing 'strange' about her is her good manners, which are severely lacking in the world today. See that you mind yours, Ethan, and you'll do just fine."

He reached for Addie again and tousled her blonde curls as she giggled at his clumsy touch. With Addie, he sometimes tried to be just "Papa" although no tender gesture came easily for him, even with this little girl he loved. Because of her reluctance in speech, we sometimes wondered if Addie was impaired. But several doctors told us she was merely slow in attaining verbal skills and would come along perfectly in due time. My father attributed the delay to the shock of my mother's death, and he had developed a sympathetic patience with Addie that he had never offered me.

He smiled at her now, held her hand, and tweaked her chin. But it was difficult for him. All too soon he let her go, turning to me again with a somber, apologetic tone. "You're too old to be pampered, Ethan, and too young to cause much trouble. The Mormon girl is here for Addie, mostly, but I expect you'll take to her. I suspect she's got a tender heart, and Lord knows, every motherless boy needs that."

★

The next morning Leah came, wrapped in a short, worn, woolen cape and wearing a knitted cap pulled low around her ears. Dark hair was hidden beneath it, a few stray curls escaping. When she removed the cap, the tresses, anchored by a crowning braid, fell loose and thick down her back, almost to her waist. Her smile was eager, her cheeks rosy from the cold, which followed her inside in the form of an icy breeze.

"I'm sorry about the wind," she said.

I was immediately smitten by her pretty voice and her eyes, large, brown, and full of light. At first I stared at her with curiosity, purposely searching for some strange flaw that made Sarah Willard so resistant to her. Within five seconds, I was staring at Leah Donaldson because she was so beautiful, and the attraction never wavered after that.

She carried a single bag, and Amos Willard, with his bushy side-whiskers, trailed after her, dragging a large trunk from his buggy. We all stood in the entry hall, sizing up poor Leah as if she were for sale and on display. Dubious Mrs. Kreiger, as fat as a butter churn, was probably noting the girl's slim figure, not made for heavy work, and my father found himself tongue-tied over the introductions. "Miss Leah . . . rather, Miss Donaldson," he stuttered, offering no proper welcome, "here are the children, Ethan and Addie. As I mentioned yesterday, they will be in your charge. Amos, here, tells me you're up to the task, and those are my expectations."

Leah nodded, flinching almost imperceptibly at his directness, and we all stood there like dolts, waiting for someone to speak. Addie saved the moment by suddenly flying toward the new arrival with open arms, clasping her and burying her face in the stranger's long, full skirt. Miss Donaldson immediately dropped to Addie's level and cupped my sister's cheeks, laughing joyously as she lightly kissed Addie's forehead. "What a little angel you are!" she cried, drawing Addie to her a second time and leaving all of us reassured about the new situation. I watched, wishing I were four again and free, as Addie was, to lose myself in Leah's soft embrace.

"Now here's a fine young man," she said, noticing me and rising up to give me her full attention, even as Addie clung to her. "Ethan, is it? We'll be good friends, Ethan. I'm counting on you to help me get acquainted with this home, this town, and"—she shot a glance at my father—"with all that's expected of me."

At that moment I was ready to slide my arm through hers and whisk her through the house as if she were a new bride coming across the threshold. Instead, I stifled the urge and simply said, "Yes, ma'am." After Leah removed her cape and gloves and exchanged a few more pleasantries, it was Addie who took her hand, leading her off with Mrs. Kreiger to explore the second floor, where her room would be, leaving me to listen to my father tell Amos Willard that if the girl didn't work out, Willard would be the one taking her back to Iowa.

"Oh, she'll work out all right," declared Amos. "If I were twenty years younger, I'd be in love with her, and I've known her not a month."

"No wonder your wife chased her away," chided Father with a smile. "She probably sensed as much." They had strolled into the parlor, where the liquor was kept, and I guessed Amos wouldn't be leaving before the two of them had tipped the brandy glasses.

"No, jealousy wasn't the problem," continued Willard, settling himself in the nearest chair and rubbing his famous whiskers. "I'm not gonna be makin' a fool of myself over a young thing such as that, and Sarah knows it." He raised his eyebrows and chuckled amiably. "But you, Pace, you have far less years than me and a clear path, should you want to take it."

My father finished filling the glasses and forced a smile. "She is a beauty," he agreed. "A man would have to be blind not to notice that." He then turned solemn as he gulped his liquor. "But she's also an orphan and a house servant with no family name—and still considerably younger than I am, Amos, no matter what you're thinking."

"And a Mormon too, which was Sarah's annoyance with her," added Willard.

"I've no objection there," replied my father, looking at the liquor bottle. "Though the girl herself would probably be put off by my ways if she's thoroughly indoctrinated."

"That she is," said Willard.

Father turned thoughtful and toyed with his glass. "The war is my mistress now, I'm afraid. Until that's over, I can't deal with encumbrances. The children are enough."

I might have flinched at the last remark, but I was still thinking of Leah and barely heard him. He must have forgotten I was even in the room. I had developed a habit of lingering in corners and shadows, eavesdropping on adults, eagerly listening for any news about the war, anxious to feel danger from a distance and leave my childhood behind. That day things were different though. For a brief moment in the entry hall, Leah Donaldson had made me wish I were a kid again, needing her attention, and I couldn't shake the thought.

I usually hung on my father's every word when he had company. Busy with their brandy and their opinions, the men in my father's parlor always drifted into rousing conversations about battles, blood, and politics, and I had a front-row seat to all this drama. Now I found myself just as interested in what a Mormon was and why Sarah Willard wouldn't like one. I wanted to know everything about this new young woman—where she came from and how long she would stay. For me, she was a sudden, all-encompassing distraction, and the politics could wait.

I knew nothing about women. Girls my own age were a nuisance, always chattering and flighty and poor with games. They seemed to be caught up in shallow things that didn't interest me—sewing and dolls and frilly dresses. They were hard to talk to about anything more serious than hairstyles and silly romance stories and who had won the Pretty Peach competition at the county fair. I was interested in books, like my mother had been, and in adventure. At fourteen, I was only beginning to be stirred by feminine attraction and had no notion of its effect. Until that day, the men could have talked all afternoon about Mormons and orphan girls and "clear paths" to matrimony, and I wouldn't have cared. Now I perked my ears up at such conversation, piqued by a sudden interest in this new beauty in our house.

Soon, however, my father and Mr. Willard left the topic of Leah behind and began to speak in sobering tones about the danger that was possibly imminent with the coming of spring. Armies would again be on the march, and Southern raiders like William Clarke Quantrill would bring their bands of thieves and cutthroats into Kansas, pouncing without warning on our military trains and supply stations, wreaking havoc in our villages, burning, looting, and killing civilians. This was usually heady stuff for a boy of fourteen. And it was personal. My father was no Jayhawker—a Kansas extremist who had used mob violence against secessionists before the war—but he was known for his Free-Soil convictions. Quantrill's murdering Bushwhackers remembered with a vengeance those who had stamped their names on the side of abolition, as my father had, and they targeted prominent men with their brand of violence.

Lawrence was considered relatively safe. The town was large and had a military presence in the form of a recruiting station and local militia. We sympathized with our vulnerable neighbors in more rural communities, and our men were full of vinegar in their behalf. But we felt secure in our own position. Warnings were occasionally issued and our militia faithfully practiced its drills, so only a few alarmists like Amos Willard worried very much.

So now, when Willard began his familiar grousing over the false security of our town and the warnings about Bushwhackers that went unheeded, I barely heard him. "If you cry wolf too often, no one pays attention anymore," he told my father in the parlor. "I fear folks will only listen with half an ear this spring."

I was listening with half an ear that day, waiting eagerly for our new governess to return from the second floor.

★

That evening at the dinner table, while Mrs. Kreiger served us, my father made an effort to get better acquainted with Leah Donaldson. She was appropriately reserved, but her smile was quick and eager when the opportunity arose. She wore a pretty lace-cuffed dress with rosebud print that was clean and pressed. With the cap and cape gone and her long hair loosely combed and accented by a single braid, Leah's smooth skin and rosy cheeks were on display, and Father seemed entranced, as silent as Addie, before he finally spoke. "Willard tells me you've been to school and know something of the classics and the sciences as well. You seem a mite young to have had all that learnin'. May I inquire further as to your situation?" My father, oddly enough, was fumbling nervously with his napkin.

"I've been fortunate in my education." Leah smiled, her hands and fingers long and graceful by her plate. "My parents died during the exodus of our people. I was six years old and taken in by a professor and his family of Mormons who remained in Iowa, hoping to eventually go west. The wife was very ill and unable to travel. While we waited for her recovery, my foster father became attached to a private school in Council Bluffs, and I was educated there, once the primary grades were behind me."

"You *are* well-spoken," observed my father. "Perhaps you had more in mind for yourself than . . . than being a children's tutor."

Leah hesitated, the smile still on her lips, and glanced at me and Addie. "Why, sir," she said lightly, "I can think of no better position than to be with children such as these."

My father cleared his throat again and nodded. He was plainly impressed with our new governess. Addie looked silently at Leah with an expression of wonder, and I lowered my chin to keep from staring. We were all taken with the girl's pleasant tone and dancing eyes.

"You have brothers and sisters back in Iowa, then?" asked my father. "Youngsters who will miss you?"

I swallowed hard. I hadn't considered we might not have Leah's undivided allegiance.

But Leah confessed, to my great relief, "Actually, my second family is gone now too—the parents dead, the grown children scattered. I am on my own again, it seems. My goal is to work my way toward the Utah Territory, where my people settled, although it may take years to get there."

"Utah Territory?" said my father. "Salt Lake City?"

"It's our Zion. Someday I hope to call it home."

I was a dreamy fourteen-year-old and as mesmerized by Leah's words as I was by her. What was this place she spoke of that anchored so many of her dreams? What kind of western desert would lure this tender beauty? I was caught up in Leah's mystery: her strange religion, her status as a wanderer, her willingness to come to Kansas in the midst of a guerrilla war.

My father seemed affected as well. "I don't know how much Willard told you about our troubles here. Perhaps he should have warned you more strenuously that eastern Kansas is a battlefield. Iowa and points north may be free from actual combat, but we here in this region are sometimes subject to raiders and outliers—*Bushwhackers*, we call them—close to Missouri as we are. They can be very dangerous."

"Mr. Willard told me that Lawrence was completely safe," replied Leah, "but even if it weren't, I think I would have come. I need the work. And with Mrs. Willard's rejection . . . I'm more than grateful for your kindness in giving me a place."

Father was quick to reassure her. "Lawrence *is* safe. I wouldn't leave my children here if I doubted that, and I wouldn't leave you with them, Miss Leah, if I doubted *you*. Sarah Willard's bigotry has worked to our advantage."

There was a light in my father's eye and a quickness in his step as he led Leah on a tour of the house after dinner. I followed along, a willing shadow, as he proudly pointed out domestic details he probably hadn't cared about in months. He even helped her tuck Addie into bed and took new pleasure in doing so, showing off his paternal warmth by twirling Addie around her toy-cluttered bedroom in her nightgown, helping her with her prayers, and smothering her with kisses until she giggled into her pillow. "My baby girl!" he exclaimed. "At last she'll have someone to talk to."

Leah enjoyed the tour as well. She responded eagerly to each nook and corner Papa showed her, and when they'd put Addie to bed, she gazed at my sister's pretty little face against the pillow and exclaimed, "What a beautiful child she is!"

Addie dimpled at the praise and watched with fascination as Leah began to fold her clothes and then bent to turn down the lamp, already taking up her duties. She waited for a moment, and when the room grew dark, Leah moved away from the bed and whispered to my father, "Is she always this quiet, or is she simply hesitant with strangers?"

"Speech has come slowly to her," he explained, looking toward Addie. "I think it's just a woman's voice she needs to hear and copy."

My father seemed to need a woman's ear. Once Addie was asleep, he lost no time directing Leah to the parlor, where he let loose a stream of pent-up sentences, hardly giving anyone else a chance to speak, delighting in a mostly one-sided conversation that filled the room with a bellowing I hadn't heard since before my mother died. Leah responded as an eager listener, nodding in agreement and occasionally commenting, though I couldn't guess why she'd be interested. My father was rejoining his regiment in the morning, and with that imminent departure on his mind, he began to speak of battle strategy and camp discipline and a thousand other things important to soldiers. Leah hung on his every word, her chin up, her dark hair flowing down her back.

"My unit is presently encamped near Fort Leavenworth, fifty miles to the north," he told her. "The first spring thaw will send the troops into action against the Southern armies in Tennessee or Georgia, and we're itching to get back into the fray."

"I imagine so," said Leah.

"Our eastern counties would probably be better served if we could stay at home and defend our people, but the folks in Washington keep pushing us to be aggressive." My father rambled over the matter, pacing the floor while Leah sat politely watching him and I stood by watching her. "I'm inclined to agree with the strategy," he repeated. "Our local citizens will have to defend themselves. I'm not too worried on that account, certainly not here in Lawrence. We are a large town, and these criminals are cowards when it comes to who they target. They'll pick on the isolated station stop or the solitary farmer and leave the larger towns alone. We could expend men to patrol the villages, but the Federal army is better off on offense, relentlessly driving and attacking the traitors at every opportunity, and the Fourteenth Kansas will always be a part of that if I have anything to say about it. Though protective defense is important, mind you, I'd sooner be on the attack when it comes to soldiering."

"Keeping the Rebels on the run will surely keep them away from Kansas," said Leah, seeming to know her cue, "and thus accomplish both your purposes."

"Right you are!" exclaimed my father. "Right you are!"

Leah Donaldson, this young stranger in our house, let my father rail on, sensing perhaps that he needed to vent. She won me over each time she shot a wink in my direction, letting me know she was aware that I was in the room whether Father was or not.

"I serve with a fine army," Father declared, "loyal men who fight for the Union and for Kansas, to say nothing of the poor black man who's been wrongfully enslaved. I hope you share my sentiments in that regard, Miss Donaldson."

"I'm very familiar with the plight of oppressed people, Mr. Pace, and I admire that your army's fighting for a righteous cause. Hopefully, the war will end soon for all of us."

"You *do* impress me, Miss Leah," replied my father, suddenly turning quiet and becoming more personal. "I'm beginning to be glad Amos brought you down from Iowa."

"And that Mrs. Willard wouldn't let me in her house?" said Leah impishly, and we all smiled at the remark.

Sarah Willard is a fool. Under my breath, I repeated my father's line and thanked God for Mrs. Willard's stupid prejudice. Leah Donaldson was ours.

Chapter Two

THE NEXT MORNING WHEN FATHER reached down from his saddle to bid us all good-bye, I noticed that he took Leah's hand in a gallant gesture. "I've only just met you, Miss Donaldson," he said, "but somehow it eases my heart to know you're here with Ethan and Addie. They'll do well in your charge. God bless you, girl."

Leah was slow to let him go, understanding perhaps more than we did the seriousness of the occasion. The war was sending countless fathers home with missing limbs or ghastly wounds, and many there were who never returned at all. But as he bid us good-bye that morning, his fine horse, Lightning, loaded with supply bags over its flanks, I had no fear about his safety. In a month, a season, a year, perhaps, I knew he'd return in glory, and I'd stand beside him, proud to be his son.

We, Addie and I, always imagined him riding into danger, but it never crossed our minds that he might not survive. We had parted like this many times, my father with his back to us, Lightning moving slowly down the road, us waving from the porch. My mother used to remain at that exact spot, watching long after rider and horse were out of sight. She'd lean forward, stare into the morning breeze, and sometimes tousle my hair as I stood by her side. She'd take Addie in her arms and say a prayer, all the while watching, hoping to catch a final glimpse of my father on some distant hill before he disappeared.

I was old enough to see the crossways of things when Mother died at home in her own bed while Father came unscathed from every distant battle. I'd call it irony today; back then, it was just cruel fate. It always led me to believe that my father was the safe one in the family, armed and guarded and surrounded by an entire regiment to protect him. My mother was the fragile one, after all, and as sure a victim of the war as any soldier at the front.

I thought of my mother as we stood that day with Leah on the porch, and I prayed to God that this new woman in our lives wasn't just as vulnerable.

★

Lawrence is situated amid the gentle hills and pastures of Douglas County, between the Kansas and Wakarusa Rivers. It was a peaceful setting for a town, with trees, fields, dusty country roads, and its village center, complete with cobbled streets and banks and liveries and churches. In spite of the pastoral atmosphere, the town had faced danger and violence before. Lawrence was sacked in 1856 by proslavery marauders angry about Kansas being admitted to the Union as a Free State and tipping the balance of power. No lives were lost, but newspaper presses were destroyed, and homes and businesses were burned.

We were proud of how the town had risen from the ashes. I was anxious to show Leah the Eldridge Hotel, a prominent landmark, and the shops along Massachusetts Street, our main thoroughfare. I wanted her to see the Congregational church where my parents had been married, and Colby's Barn, where dances were held on summer nights. Most of all, I wanted to walk with her along the river and show her what I could do with a fishing pole when the bluegills were biting.

It was still cold and blustery when she came that February, and for a while we were housebound, anxious to stay close to the fire. But this didn't stop my dreaming. Before the first week was out, I had already made plans for spring picnics and pony rides and Sunday excursions to the lake. I wanted Leah to fall in love with Lawrence so she wouldn't want to leave. I had no inkling of Salt Lake City or Utah or Deseret and why they meant so much to her. *Zion* was a foreign word.

"What is Zion?" I'd asked her that first day as she walked about with Addie and me, taking in her new surroundings. We braved the weather to show her our frosty fields and snow-topped fence posts and the stable.

"Zion? Why, Zion is the promised land."

"I've never heard of such a place."

We were all bundled up against the raw February air, and Addie's arms were tight around Leah's neck. Their cheeks were rosy, and I could see Leah's warm breath as she spoke. "It's more a state of mind than an actual place, Ethan. That's what Zion is."

I didn't know what she meant, and I was determined to ask again, but just then I was too caught up watching her laugh over Addie's efforts to cuddle closer. It was I who had insisted on the walk, anxious for Leah to see our place, and she had agreed in spite of the weather, saying the fresh air wouldn't hurt us. We kept it short for Addie's sake, but I saw that Leah had no fear of a little wind if braving it made me happy. Never had I felt more warm and contented than when I was in her presence, this girl with long dark hair and a single braid that looked so pretty in its place.

There were also folks in Lawrence I wanted Leah to meet. I was sure she'd like Mrs. Collins, who ran the mercantile, and Nancy Ford, who clerked for her father at his land claims office. Mary Carpenter, the young judge's wife, was prominent in town and had known my mother. She was pretty and always smiling. She and Louis Carpenter had been married just the past October, and he was so well respected as the local magistrate that folks already spoke of him as the next state attorney general. There was also Boneta Freeman, the schoolmaster's daughter. These people had gone out of their way to be kind to me and Addie when our mother died, and I liked them.

It didn't occur to me that any of my mother's friends might share Mrs. Willard's silly objections toward Leah. Sarah Willard was an old scissorbill, and everybody knew it. She had a way of puckering her mouth at the slightest grievance. We children gave her a wide berth just to avoid her constant censure. Our housekeeper, Mrs. Kreiger, could be vexing too, but she could never equal Sarah Willard for just plain orneriness. That woman took the prize where pucker was concerned.

Mrs. Kreiger didn't live with us. She and her white-haired husband, George, had a cottage on the back road that cut through our field and ran to town. Old George, shabby as last year's scarecrow, could be depended on to do the outside chores in my father's absence. He fed the horses, made sure our wood supply was adequate, and lent his hand to household repairs. I suppose my father worried less about us knowing there was a man nearby to look after things. Truth be told, George Kreiger was a crusty old crow who paid us scant attention. He went through the motions of his work but had no heart for it. His wife's scolding kept him faithful in his daily labors, but he disappeared whenever he could, losing himself in a bottle while he roamed the streets and alleys of Lawrence to escape her wrath. Still, I liked George. He'd lost most of his teeth, and he used to laugh at me—his mouth all gums and a sunken chin—when I tried to harness the buggy horse or saddle the tall bay on my own. I wanted George to meet Leah too and see that we had a graceful woman in the house again so he wouldn't show up drunk and acting foolish.

Most of all, I wanted Leah to meet my best friends, Bobbie Martin and Henry Kettle. Henry was black, but that didn't matter. The three of us had ruled the trails and side roads of Lawrence since we were old enough to walk. Henry had a wide grin and skin the color of molasses. He used to stick his big toe in our beehive, hoping to pull out a glob of honey before he got stung. He succeeded a time or two, and even when he didn't, he laughed about it. "It's just a bitty bee," he'd say. "No harm in that."

Bobbie and I thought he was crazy, and once when his big toe had swollen like a plum from the abuse the bees had given it, Bobbie nicknamed him Toe-Jam, or sometimes just plain Toe. The title stuck.

"It's a better name than Henry," confirmed old George Kreiger, "'specially for a boy." I admired Bobbie for his creativity and hoped someday he'd think of a swell nickname for me, although I wasn't going to stick my toe in a beehive to make him do it.

More than anything, Bobbie Martin, blond as the Kansas sun, wanted to be a soldier like his father, who had been severely injured while training with his regiment early in the war. Isaiah Martin was crippled now, so Bobbie spent hours making up for what his father couldn't do around the house, and I admired him for it. He was slightly younger than Henry and I but strong and sturdy, taller than I was by half a head and full of wanderlust. When we were kids, it was Bobbie who led out, teaching me and Toe-Jam all the things he'd learned about the creeks and caves and secret hideaways along the river. He knew the best fishing holes and where to find bird nests and even where the best bucks could be chased come hunting season.

Bobbie's talent for tracking took on new meaning once the war began. We were too young to remember it, but we'd all been taught about the raid of 1856 and were determined with boyish bravado to keep the city safe. If we heard of any irregulars snooping around Lawrence in the summer, the three of us would sneak off and look for strangers in the woods or on the backcountry trails that led the way to Topeka or Kansas City. The adults paid us little attention, and it was mostly fun and games as we pretended to be on guard should a gang of raiders come creeping anywhere near town. Bobbie was always alert and on the prowl even though we never saw anything suspicious. "Keepin' an eye out for Bushwhackers is my best game," Bobbie bragged. "No Quantrill's gonna get past me."

Bobbie made it a point to learn all he could about our most infamous enemy. He knew that William Clarke Quantrill used to live in Lawrence. He knew Quantrill had been run out of Kansas in 1860 and become a legend, leading his raiders across the border from Missouri to attack Union patrols, rob mail pouches, and damage telegraph lines. Bobbie also knew Quantrill was no hero even if some secessionists labeled him as such. In 1862 Quantrill and his raiders burned a bridge over the Blue River near Kansas City and killed the toll keeper in front of his young son. They destroyed a newspaper office in Olathe that same year, killing three civilians in the process. Just that past October, Quantrill and 150 men had swept into Shawneetown, only forty miles east of us, and surrounded a line of federal supply wagons, killing fifteen drivers and escort soldiers before ransacking the town. They were a bloody bunch, the Quantrill gang, hiding behind the Rebel flag. Even some Southerners had no use for them, ruthless as they were. Confederate General McCulloch compared Quantrill's conduct to that of a "wild savage," and several Rebel officers said the same.

"Quantrill will never come near Lawrence," our pastor, Solomon Snyder, assured us every Sunday. "He preys upon the helpless. We're too strong for his hit-and-run tactics, and God is with us as a blessed people."

Bobbie listened to Pastor Snyder—at least as much as any restless boy pressed into a pew on Sunday—but it wasn't enough to smother his determination. He always remained alert for any mischief as we boys tramped the boundaries of our world. "I'll be the first to spot 'em," he was constantly saying. "I got an eagle eye." Somehow, I knew Leah would like Bobbie and Toe-Jam, although she would probably call Toe-Jam "Henry" and leave the nickname for less cultured tongues.

Of course, there were a few citizens of Lawrence I hoped Leah never came across. One was Lonnie Hodge, a foul-mouthed, ugly, dog-snouted man who worked for Rand Saugus, whose property bordered our pasture on the north. The Jayhawkers had chased Saugus out of town because he was pro-slave and had some money and influence. A lot of prominent men on both sides vanished in those days, slipping into the shadows for their own protection. Saugus was one of them. He'd left Lonnie Hodge to mind his place while he was on the run, knowing Hodge would relish the chance to maintain a nasty presence there while steering clear of the Jayhawkers, who were after bigger fish.

Hodge hated us boys and would just as soon spit at us as offer us a cheerful word. A blatant bigot, Lonnie didn't try to hide his scorn for coloreds and abolitionists. Locally there were a few others of his stripe, but since Lawrence was known as a Free-Soiler town, no one paid them much attention. Our power was in our numbers. With the war and all, most colored-haters kept a low profile. Not Lonnie Hodge. "The state's gone to the devil!" he'd yell whenever he got drunk. "It's been taken over by blue-bellies and runaway slaves."

He may have been half right about the fugitives. Our town was once a prominent station on the Underground Railroad, and as it became more and more abolitionist, a lot of black folks on the run simply settled down in Lawrence. That's how Toe-Jam's family had arrived, coming up from Arkansas. Lonnie Hodge didn't like the situation, but he had no power, except for the sting of his tongue, and folks more or less put up with him because he was more of a nuisance than a threat. We all felt his wrath from time to time when he was drunk, but we were used to him. He was a familiar sight in town, working the various farms, hauling freight, and generally cursing the world along with his horses. It was as if he was mean for no good reason and liked messing with folks who were happier than him—which was nearly everybody. Boys like us, who were young and free to ramble and scurry about, got under his skin. I can see now that he was jealous of our place in Lawrence, sons of abolitionists as we were.

He was especially cruel to Toe-Jam, casting slurs at him and telling him he oughta be sold downriver where his kind belonged. More than once on our way to or from school, Hodge lay in wait for us, watching to see if we'd try to snag a pheasant on his boss's land or gather a few discarded wood blocks from Thatcher's sawmill. "It's that thievin' little colored kid who's teachin' ya to steal," he'd yell at me and Bobbie. "His soot is smearin' off on both of you!"

Most of all, there was something about how Hodge looked at women that made me hope he'd never get within a yard of Leah Donaldson. Even when he held his tongue, Hodge had a smarminess I didn't like. I wanted to warn Leah about Lonnie, but I didn't know how. Then one night at dinner, George Kreiger did it for me. "We got riffraff here the same as anywhere," the old man said. "But ol' Lonnie is the worst. You keep clear of him, and you'll be better off. He's trouble to good people like yourself, that Lonnie Hodge," repeated George, carelessly stirring his second cup of coffee.

"I hear the Jayhawkers are after his boss, Rand Saugus," put in Greta Kreiger. "Maybe he's the one we ought to be afraid of."

"Yeah, he's a devil too." George nodded. "Only, Hodge is the devil that's *here*."

"You're going blind, George Kreiger," objected Greta. "I still see ol' Saugus sneaking around from time to time. He stays low, but he's keeping an eye on his place. You can be sure of that."

"Well, I ain't seen him, and I'm glad of it."

Leah took all of this in with an amused expression. "Thank you for warning me about the men I need to keep the children clear of," she said.

I was glad the Kreigers liked Leah enough to warn her about Lonnie Hodge and Rand Saugus. While my father was gone, George and Greta ate supper with us every night. At least Greta did, and George came in if he was sober. He seemed to show up more often after Leah arrived, less obnoxious and with his hair slicked back.

It was funny how Leah affected people that way. Nearly everyone became more polite and pleasant, liking Leah the moment they met her. I noticed Amos Willard still smiling puppylike over her at church, while old Sarah Willard sat next to him in the pew, keeping her chin in the air and her Bible in her lap.

The city fathers, Mr. Dix, Mr. Bell, and even Mayor Collamore, all tipped their hats and gave Leah every courtesy. Their wives fawned over her as well, recognizing a kind and friendly face, a lovely addition to the women's groups in Lawrence. Unlike Mrs. Willard, most of the women didn't mind that Leah was a Mormon. I think it made her beauty less of a threat to them. She was religiously devout, whatever she called herself, and that meant she wasn't going to flirt with their husbands even while some of them mooned over her from a distance. She took up right away with Mary Carpenter and her husband, who welcomed her cordially. I think the Carpenters enjoyed Leah's intelligent conversation, rare in a young governess, I suppose. Once she got to know a few people, Leah began to socialize in a high-spirited way. The Carpenters became frequent guests at our house, especially Mrs. Carpenter, who seemed to delight in Leah's company.

"Oh, Leah," I heard Mary Carpenter once exclaim, "I'm going to send Louis to the district court in Topeka and find you a lawyer for a beau. They make marvelous husbands, lawyers do. Just ask me!" The couple had been married only a few months and still fawned over each other the way newlyweds sometimes do.

I was glad Leah was included in their circle.

Chapter Three

As I FACED THE WIND with Bobbie that February and March, meeting
Toe-Jam by the fence post on Harrow Road and making our way to
school with our mufflers pulled tight against the cold, I would catch
myself thinking about Leah. Rather than searching for rabbits or snow
owls after class, I was more and more willing to let Bobbie and Toe-Jam
run off to the ice pond or romp with Toe-Jam's dog around the willow
fields without me, though at first I didn't want to tell them why. The
truth was, I wanted to see what Leah had in mind for "culture hour,"
a session she conducted with me and Addie nearly every afternoon.
Learning was a game to Leah, and even Addie got caught up in the
stories of ancient kings and heroic battles and common folk who were
noble in simple but important ways. We had a well-stocked library, and
I knew my mother treasured books, especially the classics. She had read
to us a little, gearing most of the stories toward Addie, although I still
liked to listen. I'd lost interest when she died. The familiar sound of her
voice was gone, and that had been part of the beauty of it all. I figured
I'd give up on the great authors until I was old enough to discover
them for myself. Then Leah came along, and a lovely voice brought the
musty pages back to life again.

I liked the tales of noble Camelot and the lusty Beowulf as Leah
told them. She introduced us to Puck and Bottom and all the mis-
chievous fairies in *A Midsummer Night's Dream*. I learned that "all the
world's a stage" and "the course of true love never did run smooth,"
and the language entranced me when Leah read. I figured Bobbie
would laugh at me for that, so I began to make excuses about why I
needed to go home right away. George was drunk again, and I had

to take up the slack, or Addie was sick and Leah and Mrs. Kreiger required an extra hand. Anything to keep him from wondering. Bobbie thought governesses were for sissies once a fellow was past the age of nine or ten, and I'd agreed with him until Leah came along. But I needn't have worried. I let it out one time that Leah was helping me make a kite, and Toe-Jam and Bobbie wouldn't stay away. After that, I realized I'd been holding them back for no good reason. Soon they both fell under Leah's spell, and the five of us formed an alliance that the world might envy.

Leah wasn't all classic tales and dusty tomes. She knew parlor games that left us laughing and songs that made us dance. While she tapped out a lively tune on the piano, I would whirl a giggling Addie in my arms and "step out" like a prince. It was healing to have music in the house again.

The boys didn't take to Leah's dancing lessons particularly, but they were always there in a flash when she accompanied Addie and me outside to roust about the fields or go riding behind Old Monk in our trap. "The fresh air is good for you," she told us, "and so is the March sun when you can find it." Leah was good at driving Old Monk while being easy with the whip, but she'd often let one of us take the lines.

She paid particular attention to Bobbie's tracking instincts. "You're amazing, finding that rabbit like you did," she'd say, or, "I'm going to hire you someday to help me find the road to Zion! That way, I won't get lost!"

Before he left, Pa had designated our frisky buckskin Taffy as Leah's saddle pony, and she made good use of him, always ready for a race if Bobbie and Toe-Jam came mounted, a race she'd usually win once she caught the rhythm of Taffy's gallop. She wasn't afraid to straddle the horse, and her long skirts fell almost to the stirrups on both sides and billowed up some when Taffy hit full stride. I thought it was a beautiful thing, though some of the Lawrence ladies might have arched their eyebrows over it.

"She's a firecracker!" said Bobbie once when we were alone. "Your Leah's more of a kid than a stodgy old bitty like most governesses are. You lucked out, Ethan, and so did me and Toe. Leah can belong to all of us until some dashing soldier comes along to steal her, and don't think that won't happen. My pa says it always does."

Bobbie liked to tease, especially when it came to girls, and I seldom took him seriously. But sometimes I'd look at Leah and wonder if she worried about being in Kansas when she could have been back in Iowa or even in her Utah Zion, which she spoke of with such longing. "Someday," she'd tell us, "when I'm no longer needed here, I'll head west and find my people." I hated hearing that.

"I think Addie will always need you," I told her once, and she looked at me straight on and smiled but didn't reply.

Addie took to Leah like a new puppy. Her large eyes followed Leah's every move, it seemed, as she laid out her daily projects, helped Mrs. Kreiger with the cooking, fixed a new bonnet, or chose books from my father's library. Addie began to speak more frequently now that Leah was around. Leah conducted a "session" with her every day, where just the two of them would practice sounds and sentences. It was still a one-sided effort, for the most part, with Addie listening and merely nodding her head when asked to repeat something. "It's all right," Leah would say. "We'll keep at it, won't we, Addie, and you'll answer by and by." My sister would giggle and look into Leah's face as if she would do anything in the world to please her.

In those first weeks, we did hear a sentence from Addie, one she repeated each time Leah left the house or even the room. "Where is Leah going?" she would whisper, sometimes with alarm, sometimes with gaiety, but always with sincere wonder. Addie and Leah became connected in a way that made me envy their attachment even while I thanked God it was strong and growing.

Leah loved to role-play with us, and when the weather was too forbidding, we'd gather in the parlor for after-school romps, performing stories she'd created from great books. My favorite was *Uncle Tom's Cabin*, which Leah renamed "Ethan Pace's Parlor," written by Harriet Beecher *O'Donaldson*. Addie made a perfect Little Eva, all ringlets and cherub cheeks and no lines to learn. Toe-Jam was George, the hero, and Leah played Eliza, waving from the ice flow, her baby in her arm, as she forged the treacherous river. The "baby" was actually Addie's doll, the raging river was two sliding bars of painted waves that Toe-Jam pushed and pulled behind the scene, and the pieces of ice were a dozen pillows on the floor that Leah had to trudge through with vicious hounds and a villainous Simon Legree hot on her trail.

This was no shabby production. Leah made masks for everyone, with snouts and bulbous cheeks and bushy eyebrows. I was the old slavemaster Legree, as dastardly as ever, and Bobbie was the hound because no one could bark and growl and gnash his teeth like Bobbie could and have such fun doing it. We moved through the scene a dozen times, Leah wailing, Bobbie growling, and me acting dastardly, all in the best of fun.

We did another scene where Little Eva dies, and I was the angel who lifted her to heaven. Addie went limp and deathlike in my arms without any prompting, pleased that she didn't have to speak.

"We can't do this play without Topsy," Leah told us. So she spent an hour making ribboned braids of yarn for Toe-Jam and teaching him to say, "I 'spect I's the wickedest chil' in the whole world!" with proper sauciness.

"Look at you!" teased Bobbie, thrilled to see Toe-Jam in braids. "I'll bet your mama didn't know she had no girl!"

"I'll bet your mama didn't know she had no hound dog neither," Toe-Jam retorted with a grin, pulling on Bobbie's homemade snout until his nose got pinched.

We lay on the carpet and laughed when it was all over, even Leah, who knew more than the rest of us about the real meaning of the story. She kept a quiet smile, even when she spoke seriously about the real Harriet Beecher Stowe and how her book had changed the country. "President Lincoln called her 'the little lady who started the big war,'" said Leah. "Her story taught people about the evils of slavery. Mostly it reminded folks that people of other races or religions are just like the rest of us down deep. They have the same joys and sorrows, the same desires for freedom and happiness. Some of them are mean, some of them are sad, some are gentle, and some are funny, just like us."

"Toe-Jam's funny," said Bobbie, "'specially in his braids!"

"Not as funny as you in that hound-dog snout!" Toe-Jam's eyes were wide and good-natured.

But there was another side of it as well that Toe-Jam and Bobbie never saw because they didn't know that Leah was a Mormon. Nights alone with Leah after my friends departed and Mrs. Kreiger had gone home, I'd ask her about her strange religion and why some folks were afraid of it. We'd sit by the fire, Leah nestled against a pillow in the corner of the sofa with a shawl across her lap and me in my father's favorite overstuffed rocker, trying to figure out the mystery in this older girl. Sometimes Addie would be there, wrapped in Leah's arms, looking up wide-eyed and silent as Leah spoke or sang or simply listened. But most often I'd save my questions until Addie was in bed and I could talk more like a man to Leah.

"Papa says you Mormons were treated no better than runaway slaves once upon a time." I began this conversation hesitantly one evening when Leah seemed especially pensive. "You got run out of your homes in Missouri and Illinois. Your prophet got murdered. That's what Papa told me. Were you part of that? Did your folks suffer for their faith, like Papa says?"

"No more than most," answered Leah quietly. She was lovely there in the amber light of the parlor, soft and fragile, her long hair loose on her shoulders. "A lot of people have been persecuted at one time or another. It's the way of things sometimes. Hopefully, those that suffer do it for a righteous cause."

I wouldn't be put off. At that moment Leah was the most important thing in the world to me, and the thought of her and her family facing danger was more than I could bear. "Why was there any suffering at all?" I asked her. "Burning, killing, looting—Pa said you Mormons suffered all of that. Why did anyone take notice of what church you went to or what your prophet taught? You weren't doing anybody any harm."

She looked at me more seriously. I think she was surprised that I would care enough to ask such questions, being just a boy. But I did care. I cared because of Leah and the way she looked when she was carrying that doll and dodging pillows across our parlor floor or the way she played with us in the snow or tousled Addie's curls at night. I cared, and for the first time she could tell I cared, and so she spoke with a new intensity.

"My parents and my two brothers and I crossed the frozen Mississippi River when we had to leave Nauvoo. I was younger than Addie is now, not quite three years old. I don't remember much except the cold and the fear and the sight of our home as we left it. The temple was there too, high on a bluff, but beautiful Nauvoo belonged to us no more."

"Nauvoo?"

"The town in Illinois where I was born."

"Were you raided by someone like Quantrill?"

"Not exactly. There was no war going on, but we weren't wanted by our neighbors, and staying would only bring more trouble."

"Your family was forced out?"

"In February of 1846. As I say, I don't remember much, mainly just the confusion and the cold."

I was awestruck. "Where did you go? What did you do?"

Leah's voice was tentative, as if she wasn't sure how much to say. "We crossed Iowa in our wagon and ended up on the other side of the Missouri River in a little place called Florence, Nebraska. We called it Winter Quarters and built a community of shacks and cabins to shelter us until we could go west."

"Were there a lot of you?"

"Oh, yes. A thousand or more at one time, and all of them hungry!" Leah smiled to herself. It seemed important to her to remain lighthearted while she told the story.

"How did you live? How did that many people survive when they had no real home?"

"Many of them didn't. The graveyard grew to be almost as big as the town. In our family, my mother was the first to go. The trek from Nauvoo had sapped her strength, and she died with 'Zion' on her lips, pleading for the rest of us to keep the faith and cross the plains without her. My brother James was next, catching a bitter cough at seven years old and never getting over it. Tim, my other brother, ate some weeds along a ditch bank and suffered terribly before he finally passed. He was ten—my father's little man. I think Pa just gave up after that. He seemed to lose whatever vitality he had."

"He still had you," I murmured.

Leah was quiet for a moment. Her eyes drifted past me and finally closed. When she spoke again, it was with a gentle smile. "My father loved me, Ethan, and he knew his body was too weak to keep on going. He knew he wouldn't last. So he made a bitter choice. He found the Abbotts, the professor's family, and arranged for them to take me as their own. I don't know what became of him. I suppose he died and is buried somewhere on the way to Zion, for he promised my mother that's where he'd go. I made that promise too, in my heart, and someday I aim to keep it."

"Why is Zion so important? What makes it so special that folks risk dying just to get there?"

Leah turned to a Bible we had lying by the lamp and found a certain page. "People are drawn to places that are sacred for one reason or another," she said. "For Mormons, the prophet Isaiah wrote of our promised land with these words: 'In the last days, the Lord's house shall be established in the tops of the mountains, and shall be exalted about the hills; and all nations shall flow unto it. And many people shall go and say, Come ye, and let us go up to the mountain of the Lord, and he will teach us of his ways, and we will walk in his paths; for out of Zion shall go forth the law, and the word of the Lord from Jerusalem.' Mormons believe that God's power has been restored on earth. That power can be used to bless us individually or as a people. For us, our valley in the mountains of the West is the second Jerusalem, the promised Zion. That's where we believers want to go, no matter how long it takes." Leah closed the book and patted it with her hand as if she'd just read poetry. I was caught up in her reverie whether I understood all the words or not.

"Why didn't you go straight there, once you grew up, instead of coming here?"

"It's a terribly long way to Zion, a thousand miles and more. I'm alone in this world, Ethan. I've got to earn the money and the means to go, but God will help me do it. I know He will if I do my part and keep my promises."

"What promises do you have to keep?"

"Well, there's lots of things, but the sum of it is I want to live a virtuous life and be worthy of the Lord's blessings, be worthy of going to Zion, so God will make it possible."

"Seems to me you're as worthy as anyone. I'll bet all your people out in Zion have plenty of faults, just like folks do here in Kansas."

"I'm sure they do, Ethan." She smiled. "But I made the Lord a special promise, a promise just between the two of us. It's one I want to keep as well as I can. You'll know better when you're older what I mean." She spoke a little nervously, as if she didn't think I'd understand. "I don't have much of value in this world, Ethan, so I pledged purity to God in exchange for His help in finding my way to Zion. The Lord would forgive me, and Zion's people would accept me with my faults, but I want to *feel* worthy of the place in my own heart and soul. Do you understand?"

"No," I answered. "Seems like you suffered for your Zion, and that should be enough."

"Well, we'll see." She straightened her shoulders and made an effort to change the direction of our conversation. Maybe she regretted getting personal, but I didn't mind.

★

One night when Addie was still up, I asked Leah what a bigot was. My father had used the term, and I thought I knew its meaning, but I wanted Leah to explain it since she had a special way of making things clear.

"Some people worry about folks who are different," she said, lifting Addie from her shoulder but speaking mostly to me. "They're threatened by things they don't understand, and when folks feel afraid, they get angry. They do things they never thought they would, especially if others goad them on. They become animals like those hound dogs chasing Eliza in the story, forgetting that they're human beings, just like the folks they're chasing."

"Toe-Jam's family had to run away from Arkansas," I said.

"History is full of folks like that." Leah nodded. "Look, I want to show you something." She rose, leaving Addie and me on the sofa, and moved toward our large stone fireplace. "Come here, Ethan. I'll need your help." She felt with her fingers around the edges of stone on one side, just under the mantle. Where a large wood panel framed the stone, she found the upper lip and carefully added pressure until the piece came creaking forward from under the shelf. "Do you know about this?"

I was astonished. "No, I never knew it came apart like that. What is it? A secret door?" I reached to help her with the panel, and Addie jumped off the sofa and stood wide-eyed and eagerly watching. This was curious fun.

"It's not exactly a door," said Leah. "But there is a small space just behind the panel and against the stone where someone could hide if he were small enough. I discovered it the other day when I was sweeping the hearth and noticed a crease there at the edge."

We looked curiously into a dark little cave. It was about two feet deep with a width of about a yard. There were dust and cobwebs at its edges, and only a small person could fit in there comfortably once the panel was closed. The idea of a secret hiding place in our own parlor sent excited shivers through me.

"It's a priest hole," said Leah, measuring the edges with a poker as we all bent to peek under the mantle. "At least, whoever built this fireplace used that pattern, probably on a whim."

"What's a priest hole?" I asked.

"Well," Leah began to explain, "it goes back to what we were talking about, how sometimes people of one religion or another are persecuted for their faith." I helped her slide the stone block and wooden panel into place again, being careful that the edges were even and the space was still our secret. "During the 1500s in England, the people in power had a dislike for Catholics," Leah continued. "Catholic priests served their followers in secret at the threat of arrest and even death. Good Catholic families who wanted a priest to perform a wedding or some other ritual sometimes had to hide the man from the English soldiers. *Priest holes* became a popular name for little secret spaces such as this."

"It's a swell thing to have right here in our parlor," I said. "I wonder if Father knows it's here. I can hardly wait to show Bobbie and Toe-Jam. Bobbie will think it's keen; that's for sure."

Leah looked at the fireplace thoughtfully and then back at me. "Ethan, I think whoever built that priest hole meant it to stay a secret. Why don't we keep it just between the three of us—you, me, and Addie—at least until your pa gets home. Let's make a promise never to speak of it again, to have something that only we three know about. What do you say to that?"

"Sure, I guess," I answered while Addie nodded vigorously. I was disappointed, though, and couldn't understand the need for secrecy when the priest hole was such a fine discovery. I studied Leah a moment as she stoked the fire up again, and then we retreated back to the sofa. "Where'd you learn all that about the 1500s," I asked, "and all about priest holes and such?"

"It comes from books about history." She shrugged. "Lectures I've heard, mostly on religious tolerance, which was personal for me."

"I've never heard of a priest hole before or that Catholics once had to hide out like you Mormons."

She picked up the book she'd made the role-play from, *Uncle Tom's Cabin*, and cradled it in her hand. "That's why reading's so important. You get to know other people, and you find out that deep down, they're a lot like you. Once you get to know a person, even in a book, chances are you like him, no matter what his color or religion is."

"Life's not always like a book," I said, eyeing the particular volume she held.

"You like Henry, don't you? He's black, but you're the best of friends."

"I've grown up with Toe-Jam. I don't really think about him being black. He's just a kid I know."

"See what I mean," said Leah.

I nodded, beginning to understand.

"And I hope you like me too," she added, smiling. "Though, being Mormon, I'm as different from you as Toe-Jam is, in a whole lot of ways."

My heart fluttered against my chest. I *did* like her, so very much, and I didn't care that she was different. Her differences—her sense of mystery, her loyalty to a strange religion—just added to her charm.

"Let's keep our priest hole a secret," Leah repeated, "if only because its purposes are thankfully in the past. It's not needed anymore." She laughed then, that happy, jubilant laugh.

Chapter Four

BOBBIE WAS STILL BENT ON "spying" once good weather began. It was partly a game, I think, but also a way Bobbie had of making up for his father's incapacity—or maybe for avenging it. Bobbie was determined to spot Quantrill or any other Bushwhacker who came sniffing around Lawrence, and this summer he planned to do it from some secret vantage point instead of casting about by chance. With time on his hands once school was out, he talked me and Toe-Jam into using a tall elm tree for our spying post. The tree was in an old seedy garden plot at the far end of Massachusetts Street. A high brick wall lined the place, and beyond it lay a forest and a small sweep of pastureland on Stony Hill above the river. A grove of old trees lined the wall, but one elm was the tallest. Drooping leaves and branches covered the bricks for several feet, and anything we built there would be easy to hide. A little cluster of bushes and trees called Detmer's Grove anchored the far end of Massachusetts Street, and the first building didn't appear for another quarter mile after that. It seemed the perfect hideaway.

Bobbie saw a way to quickly climb the elm by attaching a rope and ladder rungs to the chinked bricks of the wall. "Why, we could squirrel in there and make our ladder with no one ever seeing us," urged Bobbie. "From that leafy limb up yonder, we can watch the east road clear to the county line almost, with no one knowing we're there. Turn the other way, and we can keep an eye on home, all the while hidden from anyone we don't want to find us, Bushwhacker or not."

It seemed a simple plan, even a noble one, given our lazy summer days. Perhaps Lawrence did need its boys to keep an eye out for the enemy. Bobbie was eager enough, and pretty soon we had it made, a ladder almost to the highest branches of the tree. We gathered some castaway pieces of lumber from Thatcher's sawmill to use for the rungs and nailed them to anything firm along the wall—branches, creases in the bricks, draining spaces. We added a rope that ran from top to bottom, looping it around each rung and knotting it at the ends.

Bobbie was the first to scramble to the top once the job was done, and he called down, eager to have us join him. With Toe-Jam right behind me, I climbed the ladder and crawled out on the broad limb where Bobbie proudly sat. "Look at that." He admired the view. "No Quantrill's gonna creep past those pastures now!"

It was a magnificent scene; the fields were awash in color—corn and wheat—the river sparkled silver to the north of us, trees swaying here and there along its banks. We took in our village, too, with its familiar streets giving way to quiet neighborhoods and farms. The dirt roads leading in all directions from the town could be easily watched from this vantage point, and I admired Bobbie for his bravado and initiative even if the threat was empty, the enemy far away.

"This is keen!" I told him. "You can see forever from up here. Maybe we ought to show Mayor Collamore what we've done, tell him we'll be on the lookout every day. It just might ease his mind if he knows he's got some extra eyes up here."

"I could tell my ma I'm workin' for the man!" put in Toe-Jam. "We might get us a medal."

But Bobbie shook his head. "Naw, let's not tell anyone—except maybe Leah and maybe Addie 'cause she never says anything. Most folks would think we was foolish and only playing games. Besides, I like secrets. A secret adds a little sugar to anything you do, all the way around."

I thought of the priest hole in our parlor and nodded as Bobbie spoke. Some things were best left quiet. But I was glad Bobbie wanted to include Leah in the secret of Detmer's Grove. Secrets were even more fun if she were part of them.

But that devil Lonnie Hodge almost gave things away before we even got the chance to tell Leah about the lookout post. He'd caught us picking through the cast-off boards at the sawmill and knew we were up to something. The previous fall we'd gotten permission from the saw master, John Thatcher, to use his extra wood for a duck blind we were building. Lonnie had been full of thunder about it: "I know you little varmints! Yer tryin' to build a post for spyin' on the river. You get your carcasses out of that wood pile! Yer fools to think of seein' ol' Quantrill before he puts a long blade in yer gizzard!"

The day after we finished the ladder at Detmer's Grove, Hodge came to my house, looking as dark and ugly as a demon and carrying a rawhide buggy whip. I caught a glimpse of him, but before I could run in from the barn, he was speaking out of turn at Leah on the porch and making my blood start to boil.

"That boy of yours and them two he hangs with have been stealing wood again from Thatcher's place. That wood belongs to Rand Saugus, who owns the mortgage on the mill. I seen 'em haulin' wood toward town on a pallet sled. You tell them little thieves I got their number and Saugus has hired me to run 'em down." Scraggly and festered as an old warthog, Hodge was slapping his palm with the coiled whip. He stood eye-to-eye with Leah, who refused to back away.

"You have no proof the boys stole anything, Mr. Hodge, and I'll thank you to get off my porch!"

"Yer porch? Ha!" bellowed Hodge. "It ain't yer porch. Yer one of those dirty Mormons come beggin' from Illinois. Pace wouldn't like to know what yer doin' to his boy, I'll wager. Lettin' him hang about with that colored kid, teachin' him to steal. 'Course that's what you Mormons are famous for, ain't it? Stealin' other people's property."

"We've stolen nothing, and neither has this boy. If you come here again, you better have the sheriff with you and a warrant. Now, I'll tell you one more time, get off *my* porch."

I arrived, out of breath, just as Hodge took a step toward Leah with his whip raised and his eyes aflame. "You think I'm gonna take yer sass?" he snarled at her. "You think Rand Saugus cares about some skinny stem of a woman?"

I was ready to lunge at Hodge when Leah stepped between us, pushing me away and putting herself against the devil, who was still breathing fire.

"You think I'm afraid to touch a woman?" snorted Hodge. "You think you can hide that little varmint behind yer skirts? Why, girlie,

I could twist you like soft leather, and someday I'll do it too! No one around here would blame me neither. You Mormons are always ripe for pluckin'."

I made another move toward Hodge, and again Leah held me back while she continued to stare him down. He finally twisted his lips into another sneer and moved backwards off the porch, chortling a curse before he turned and walked away. I had no fear of him or Rand Saugus. We hadn't touched Saugus's bricks or his woodpile. This was only Hodge's way of making trouble. But Leah didn't scare easily. It must have rankled Lonnie that she didn't cringe and cower at his angry mouth and ugly threats. Looking back, I think he most likely left the porch that day feeling a little chastened and determined to lash back against this skinny stem of a girl who'd stood up to him.

I felt proud afterwards. I had jumped in to defend Leah, and even though she stopped me, she knew I would have taken a swing at Lonnie for her sake. I marched around the whole day with my shoulders back and my chin held high.

Leah knew exactly where I stood. That evening I was surprised when she scolded me a little. "Don't ever go after a grown man with your fists, Ethan. You'll catch the worst of it and end up giving the devil pleasure."

It would be worth every bruise, I thought, *and the devil's pleasure, too, if I was doing it for you.*

That evening on the sofa, with Addie cuddled against her and a book in her lap, Leah was quiet. I knew she was still thinking about Lonnie. The fire was blazing to warm a cool twilight. "Hodge had no right to speak that way," I said. "To you or anyone. And I'm not a thief." I slid into the rocker close to her and hung my head. Her reprimand, mild as it had been, had diminished some of my glory.

Leah looked at me for a moment then suddenly moved over, keeping Addie on one side of her and inviting me to take the other. "Come here, Ethan," she said. "I want to tell you a story."

At first I thought the book in her lap was the Bible, but it turned out to be something else, The Book of Mormon. It looked like scripture, the way it was printed, but I wasn't sure. I hesitated.

Leah had never shown us this book before, and there was something mysterious about it, maybe something that made Sarah

Willard reject Mormons and Lonnie Hodge curse like a devil on our porch.

"What kind of a story?" I said dubiously.

"Well, it's about a good man whose faith gave him special power against the storms of life. His name was Nephi, and once he was on a ship that was being whipped and battered about in the waves because the wicked people around him were angry. They were jealous of his gifts and angry at his righteous efforts to guide them. They tied him up and tortured him. They insulted him and his wife and children and his parents, who were all helpless against the storm. Their compass wouldn't work while Nephi was bound, and the ship pitched and rolled violently through the wind."

Addie looked up at Leah with wondering eyes, and I listened intently to the rhythm of Leah's voice, no longer worried about Saugus or Lonnie Hodge.

"Fear and panic raged through the ship because the wicked people realized the storm was getting worse and they had no compass. As much as they worked and struggled, there was no way to save the ship. In the wild storm, they would surely drown."

"They needed Nephi to help them," I said. "They needed to let him go."

"And they finally did," said Leah. "They untied his swollen wrists and ankles, and they repented of the way they'd treated him."

Addie tightened her little fists and gasped excitedly, bouncing up and down from where she sat.

"And he saved them all," I said, "somehow guiding the ship to safety."

"*How* he did it is important," added Leah, running her finger along the page in her lap. "After they loosed me, behold, I took the compass, and it did work whither I desired it. And it came to pass that I prayed unto the Lord; and after I had prayed the winds did cease, and there was a great calm . . . and I, Nephi, did guide the ship, that we sailed again towards the promised land."

We sat in silence for a moment, taking in the essence of what had been read. I thought of Leah's people, the Mormons, and how they had been persecuted and whipped about on a stormy sea, how Leah had been mocked and insulted, even here in Lawrence. It would be

Leah's faith that would save her in the end and lead her eventually to Zion, her own promised land. I caught on to the meaning of the story. Leah was telling us that God provides the compass, but the traveler has to have faith and a willingness to follow the Captain, whose ship it is. I wondered if someone would come along in Leah's life with the power to guide her to Zion and save her from the storm. Suddenly, I wanted to be that hero. But even then, I knew that if I had the chance, I'd do it with my fists and not my faith. I didn't know what faith was at the time. Leah had it, and this man Nephi had it. But I was just a kid, and Zion was just a vision—and very far away.

★

It took a while to convince Leah to survey the hideout at Detmer's Grove. She was busy, she said, doing girly things with Addie. But at last, once when she was shopping on Massachusetts Street, all dressed up in her best town bonnet and holding Addie's hand, the chance came, and I made the most of it.

I was with Bobbie in the branches of our lookout spot, leaning back and admiring the view. The leaves were green and lush, with May upon us, and they kept our hiding place well concealed. I spotted Leah and Addie in the distance looking in the shops, coming up Massachusetts Street from where they'd left the buggy. Bobbie and I scrambled down and raced toward town as fast as we could, figuring this would be the perfect time to show Leah our peeping post, as proud of it as we were. We found her and Addie in the millinery and busted in there all out of breath, almost knocking over a display rack in our rush. But Leah was forgiving, as was Mrs. Fitch, who owned the shop.

"Their angel mother will thank you one day," Mrs. Fitch told Leah as she steadied the display rack and scowled briefly at Bobbie, needing somebody else to blame. "These poor children need a firm but gentle hand."

Leah made me apologize, and I nudged Bobbie with my foot until he did the same. But we were both too excited to be all that repentant, and Leah sent a wink with her reprimand.

"We've got something to show you," I cried the minute we were all out the door. "We've been telling you about our hideaway at Detmer's Grove. Well, it's just nearby and ready for your inspection!"

"Show me!" Leah smiled at our enthusiasm and trailed along after us with Addie at her side.

I don't know why it was so important for us to share our secret with this prim young woman who was no more interested in boys' games than Addie was. Sure, she'd thrown snowballs at us and let herself be chased by make-believe hounds through a river of ice, but that was just play acting. We—Bobbie, Toe-Jam, and I—liked to think that our perched hideaway in Detmer's Grove was the real thing, an actual outpost in the war where we could risk our necks as spies and sentinels for our country. This wasn't a girly thing, yet I yearned for Leah's approval. I wanted her to realize I wasn't just a runny-nosed kid that needed her protection. Our country was at war, and I was brave enough to do my part in its defense. Bobbie was a natural show-off. He just liked to advertise. But for me, taking Leah to the grove caused my heart to pound.

"So look here," said Bobbie when we reached the end of Massachusetts Street. "You see how this path is hidden by the trees and overgrowth?" He was careful about who was watching as he pointed out our trail and led Leah and Addie into the leafy thicket.

Leah smiled and raised her skirts just above the grass. "This is exciting. Who would know this path was even here?"

"Wait till you see," I added eagerly.

I let Bobbie take the lead, and we moved through the shaded grove, heading to the place where the bluff's sharp incline began. There we pulled the brush away and proudly showed Leah the ladder we'd constructed using the rope and rung-size blocks of pine from the woodpile. We scrambled up the ladder, and I think Leah would have followed had she not been dressed for town in a full skirt and petticoats.

She nodded her approval and lifted Addie to the second rung just to hear her laugh.

"I can see forever from up here," Bobbie yelled, sitting at the highest point. Below him, I focused in on Leah's upward gaze. Suddenly, the thought that we'd be protecting Leah and Addie from the Bushwhackers with this lookout post took hold of me, and that thrilled me more than anything.

Coming down, Bobbie and I were careful to cover each ladder rung with leaves and weeds, concealing the steps and keeping them our secret. We groomed the path through Detmer's Grove to our advantage too, making our creation all the more intriguing and secure.

"At the first sign of trouble," said Bobbie, "me and Toe-Jam or Ethan are gonna climb up that hidden ladder. I'll draw a bead on whoever's comin' down the river or across from the south, and I'll send Ethan to the militia with the warning. We'll have one up on those Missourians before they can get within five miles of us. No problem at all."

"You boys are marvelous! Why, you're already heroes for your age!" Leah set her packages down, put a hand on each of our shoulders, and shook us in delight. "Your father would be proud, Ethan," she added, giving me an extra squeeze. Leah congratulated Bobbie too and said he'd done a noble thing that might one day help the town. She put her fingers to her lips and promised to keep the hidden ladder a secret for as long as she lived in Lawrence.

"It was mostly Bobbie's idea," I told Leah as we walked back to town and the waiting buggy. I was carrying the packages, which seemed as light as air.

"Yer darn right it was," said Bobbie, laughing. "I'd take on them Bushwhackers single-handed if I could."

He left us at the buggy, scrambling home the shorter way on foot, and though I liked Bobbie, that day I was glad to see him go. I wanted to take in Leah's praises by myself. Riding down our road I watched the way Leah used the lines to slap the team and how she guided Old Monk, the outside horse, so he wouldn't skirt the edge too close, as he was prone to do. Leah handled Old Monk as well as she did Taffy. I admired a woman like that, one that could handle rowdy boys and horses with equal skill. Leah really could be an asset to our little army, I decided, if she weren't a girl. I listened to her laugh there in the buggy. I noticed again her rosy cheeks and sunny smile, the way her hair fell down her back, anchored by that pretty braid. I saw the shine of those dark eyes, dancing as she talked, and I knew our army could do without another soldier. There was no way I wanted Leah to be a boy. I liked her just the way she was.

Then she said something that startled me.

"You and Bobbie and Henry have put your minds to a great thing. Being lookouts for the town is admirable even if Quantrill never shows his face."

"Olathe was raided. Blue River too," I reminded her. I was trying to prove that our ladder wasn't a child's game. We took things seriously. "You can never be too careful."

"No," said Leah, suddenly solemn. "And that's why I think Detmer's Grove is a good place for you. You stay there if trouble comes. No matter what happens, you stay hidden in those trees."

"Well, we'd have to come out with a warning." I was perplexed and a little hurt. We hadn't strung the ladder so we could hide like cowards. "Besides," I said, "I'd want to be with you and Addie if there was going to be a raid."

She nodded once. "A warning is one thing, staying out of sight and safe is something else." She pulled to a stop in front of our barn as the horses whined and tossed their heads. "You keep hidden in the grove if you're there when trouble comes. Addie and I can take care of ourselves." She cuddled Addie close to her and finally smiled at me. "But let's hope it doesn't come to that. Let's keep Detmer's Grove a game just like Simon Legree and Little Eva and all those hounds!"

★

I never told Bobbie that all our work at Detmer's Grove was just a game. And when he came marching up to our house one day in a Union-blue outfit his mother had sewn for him, I was as envious as a pauper looking at a prince. The coat had gold buttons down the front and gold bars on the shoulders. The trouser pants were striped with a gold belt buckled at the waist.

Bobbie was as proud as a peacock in his new uniform and seemed to stand a little straighter when he wore it, which was darn near every day once summer came full on. He high-stepped around our parlor showing off for Leah and Addie and said he was a real soldier now, not much younger than some of the recruits down at the federal station. There was no doubt the uniform gave him swagger.

"My ma made it from a real officer's extra duds," he told us. "It makes me feel . . . feel . . ."

"Invincible?" supplied Leah with a smile.

"Yeah, that's the word, I guess. Mighty swell, don't ya think?"

"Your ma's an excellent seamstress. You do look heroic."

We watched him take up Addie and swing her in his arms, playing the dashing lady's man as well as the gallant soldier. And we laughed when Addie's lacy pinafore got caught on the gold belt buckle, causing her to scream with delight when Bobbie couldn't put her down.

I thought the uniform was the handsomest outfit I'd ever seen, and Leah seemed to like it too, smiling and fussing over Bobbie the way she did. When he was gone I asked her if she could make me one like it if I were to come up with the cloth. I was surprised when she said no.

"I don't want you standing out that way, Ethan," she said. "If Bobbie was my boy, I'd tell him the same."

"But I thought you liked his suit," I whined. "You fussed over him well enough."

Leah shot a startled glance at me, raising an eyebrow at my tone. Then she smiled again. "But Bobbie's not my boy," she said, running her fingers through my hair. "You are."

Her words and smile melted me, to say nothing of her touch. I didn't care about the uniform anymore.

"Bobbie's suit is fine for him to march around in," said Leah, "but it may also label him a soldier when he's just a boy. War can make young boys grow up too soon."

I knew what she meant, but at that moment, standing close to her, I cursed my youth. Grow up too soon? I could never grow up fast enough.

Chapter Five

MAY TURNED INTO JUNE, AND with the rising temperatures came rising tension as national war news fired every conversation from the breakfast table to the local tavern. General Grant's army had laid siege to Vicksburg, Mississippi, after at least two direct assaults on the river port had failed. Fierce fighting leading up to Vicksburg—the Black River Campaign and the defeat of Confederate General Pemberton at Champion's Hill—had left Mississippi reeling. In the East, Robert E. Lee was marching into Pennsylvania, determined to split the North and surround Washington. Our Kansas newspapers kept us apprised of these events and the pace of every bloody battle. Federal army recruiters stuck in Lawrence claimed an itch to join the action. The "leftover" men of our militia felt old and forgotten as history passed without them on some far-off battlefield. I missed my father, but I was proud of where he was—not moping here at home and feeling useless like Bobbie's father did.

Of course, the threat of Quantrill and his raiders charging into town haunted us boys far more than Lee's advance into Pennsylvania. Bobbie, Toe-Jam, and I spent part of every day perched on the bluff at Detmer's Grove or in the Methodist church tower. Bobbie's pa, who'd never got a chance to see a real battle before his injury in training, gave us an old pair of field glasses that we fought over when it came to our lookout duties. Bobbie claimed they were his and belonged at Detmer's Grove. I figured I could make good use of them at the church tower, with the broad view it gave me of the southeast hills. After a while it didn't seem to make a difference.

June passed with no sign of Quantrill, with or without the glasses, and I let Bobbie have his way. The town fathers were right. Lawrence was too big to be a target of the fly-by-night marauders even if Quantrill hated us.

Then one afternoon, while Toe-Jam and I were rooting around an old abandoned barn on the Stoker place, I got the scare of my life and learned the war really wasn't that far away.

The roof had caved in on one side of the shed and settled on a slant. We were down under the eaves where the tack room used to be, searching through a bunch of rusted tools, as boys are prone to do, when we heard the old slat door fly open on the upright side of the barn.

Soon we saw two men shadowing the light. "What'd I tell ya about comin' here?" growled one man to the other. "Didn't I tell ya to wait till it was dark? You got no good ears to hear with, boy?"

It was Rand Saugus. I recognized his voice first, and then I could see his long, sharp chin and hooded eyes. His thin hair was slicked back under his hat. He had always seemed a silent and shadowy figure, controlled and brooding. Now he was pushing Lonnie Hodge across the straw and slapping him. "You want to bleed these fools in Lawrence, you got to mind everything I say!"

"You ain't been around to say much lately," cried Hodge, raising his elbows against the blows. "Light or dark, you ain't been around."

"You just shut up and listen." Saugus pulled back and looked suspiciously from the sagging rafters to the ancient manger. "Quantrill wants his list," he breathed. "The list I promised him."

"I ain't no good with lists," Hodge pleaded. "You know the names as well as I do or better. I'm no good with a pen."

"No, but you're good at sneakin' about, now ain't ya?" Saugus was clutching the front of Lonnie's coat. "You know the comings and goings of everyone in town. How many men and boys are left since the war took up? How many's gone off to fight and how many's left behind? Where does most of 'em gather? That's what Quantrill wants to know."

Hodge shrugged helplessly. "Most of the men that's fit enough have gone off to the war. Stephen Pace is gone. Wendell Bradley and young John Kelly. They're all Yankees now. Tim Condie and Brewster

Webb are in the Fourteenth Kansas like Pace and most of the others."
He wiped his mouth as Saugus let go of him and stepped away to
consider things. "The recruits come and go as usual," he added, "but
they're just fuzzy-cheeked kids who don't care a speck for Lawrence."

"I been braggin' up the place as ripe for pickin'," Saugus
grumbled. "Now you're tellin' me there's no one left that's worth a
Rebel bullet?"

"Mostly women and kids is all that's left."

"Quantrill says women are off limits," chuckled Saugus. "He
claims it's cowardly to strike the innocent. I say I never knew a woman
who was all that pure." He pummeled Lonnie on the shoulder in a
renewal of friendship, and I perked up my ears at the hired man's
response.

"There's a little fire-breather down at Pace's who needs to feel the
back of someone's hand. A Mormon girl, she is, and haughty as a
peacock. Thinks she owns the place since the lady of the house passed
on."

"I've seen her." Saugus nodded, staring beyond Lonnie for a
moment. "She has a pile of dark hair and rides a buckskin pony."

"That's her. She tried to throw me out one day when I came after
what was yours."

Saugus didn't seem to be listening. "Yes," he mused, still in a
trance. "I think I've seen her."

The two of them soon left the barn, and I heard Toe-Jam, who
was crouched beside me, exhale painfully. "By golly, it wouldn't be
smart to get caught in here with Rand Saugus sneakin' around." He
scrambled up before I could lay hands on him. We crept across the
straw and watched through a crack in the door as Hodge and Saugus
disappeared into the woods beyond the clearing. Beads of sweat
dripped down my back, and my hands were trembling.

We went straight to Provost Marshal Banks at the courthouse and
told him what we'd heard. Banks was a solid man with years behind
him as a local peace officer. Some folks said he was getting too old
for the job. He looked strong enough, with thick arms and legs and
a square, determined jaw, but he had a thatch of snow-white hair
and a hunch to his back that reminded people of how long he'd been
around. The war had taken the younger men, or Banks might have

been turned out to pasture long before. He listened to us amiably. "Sounds like Saugus sneaks around a lot. The old Stoker's place, you say?"

"Yes, sir. He was talking to Lonnie Hodge about a list."

"List? What kind of list?"

"It sounded like a target list for when Quantrill shows up," I said breathlessly while Toe-Jam nodded nervously beside me.

Banks rubbed his chin whiskers thoughtfully and cursed beneath his breath. He asked us to tell him all we'd seen and heard again, and then he leaned back in his chair to consider things. "You boys have had a few dustups with Lonnie Hodge, as I recall," he said suspiciously.

"That doesn't mean we didn't see him with Rand Saugus like we said!"

"No need to get your back up." Banks held up his hands. "There's no one here who's friends with that varmint Hodge nor Rand Saugus for that matter. But I'll tell ya this: I have no worries about any kind of list. Lonnie Hodge can't write his name, and Saugus wouldn't risk the Jayhawkers by showing his face in Lawrence. I want to thank you boys, but you better go back to Detmer's Grove. We could use the news if you sight an army comin', but two fellows sneakin' around Stoker's don't scare me."

I was surprised Banks knew anything about Detmer's Grove and was so taken aback it silenced me. Maybe these local lawmen were more aware than I thought.

Just then Louis Carpenter caught sight of me in the marshal's office and came in to see why I was there. He was courteous, finding me and Toe-Jam both a chair while Banks had left us standing.

"Does Miss Leah know you're here?" the young judge asked after showing great interest in our story.

"No, sir," I answered. "I don't like mentioning Lonnie to Leah. It would scare her to know he might have caught us in that shed."

Carpenter nodded, smiling. "You were right to come, Ethan. Marshal Banks will keep an eye on things."

I wasn't so sure.

At that moment Mayor George Collamore walked into the room, and Toe-Jam and I cowered a little under the weight of all the authority facing us. But the men were all solicitous even if our revelations caused no great alarm.

"I put no stock at all in Saugus's reference to Quantrill," Banks told the others. "Saugus is no vigilante. He was showing off for Hodge; that's all it was. Trying to keep Lonnie on his toes."

"What about this list the boys heard him talking about?" asked Carpenter. "What do you suppose that means?"

"Who knows?" shrugged Banks. "Could have been some business Saugus wanted Hodge to take care of on his place."

"There was more to it than that," I interrupted, trying to press my case. "They were talking about the strength of the town, how many able-bodied men were here."

"Yes, and them raiders know we got *too* many," laughed Mayor Collamore. "That's what Saugus will likely tell Quantrill if they ever do meet up this side of hell. We've got a recruiting station here. There's no way Quantrill would be foolish enough to attack Lawrence, and there's no way that reprobate Saugus even knows the captain. He was only pumping out his chest for Lonnie, like the marshal said." The mayor looked approvingly at me and Toe-Jam and reached to pat my shoulder. "Your father would be proud of you," he declared. "We're proud of you too, of both of you, and we're glad ol' Saugus didn't find you in that shed. He's a snake if there ever was one."

Following the mayor's lead, Marshal Banks stood up and extended his hand. "Thank you, boys, but I don't believe you heard anything I can use. Saugus sneaks about, scared of Jayhawkers; I doubt he's ever been within ten miles of William Clarke Quantrill."

Judge Carpenter kindly shook my hand and Toe-Jam's too. "I won't mention this to my wife or Miss Leah if you think it will disturb them." He led us to the door, his arm across my shoulder. "But you boys be careful. I've heard rumors that Saugus comes around sometimes. He's taking a chance. There are Jayhawkers who would string him up if they ever caught him. Still he comes. I don't know what he's planning, sneaking around here like he does, but he's bound to be trouble for anyone coming face-to-face with him."

Carpenter waved good-bye as we left the courthouse. We walked down the street still wondering what to do. We were silent for a while, still thinking about Rand Saugus and his ugly words. "You think we oughta tell the adjutant at the recruiting station that we seen Rand Saugus and that old Quantrill's got his eye on Lawrence?" asked Toe-Jam. He was leisurely whipping a stick through the wheat as we moved along.

"Sure, we can tell him, for what it's worth. But folks just don't believe that Saugus would be riding with Quantrill."

"Seemed like he was."

"We'll keep an eye out, but it isn't likely he'll show his face again."

"That's okay with me," muttered Toe-Jam. "That Saugus has an ugly face to see, and Hodge is right behind him."

I chuckled at Toe-Jam's description and left him at the fence post on Harrow Road where our paths split. Truth be told, I wasn't all that worried about Rand Saugus having ties to Quantrill either. It was something else that Saugus said that bothered me more. *I think I've seen her.* That's what Saugus said when Lonnie told him about Leah. *I think I've seen her.* There was something about the tone of his voice that sent a chill through me whenever I remembered it, an absence of interest in every other word that Hodge was saying. It still haunted me that next day as I walked home across the fields. *I think I've seen her. She has a pile of dark hair and rides a buckskin pony.* I remembered Saugus's words about Leah, and Quantrill was an afterthought from that time on.

★

I was becoming more caught up than ever in what Leah had in mind that summer. She seemed determined to "rescue our childhood," and though she cautioned us about what to do if trouble came and continued to praise Bobbie for his efforts as a lookout, she guided me and Addie toward less serious pursuits. We rode the saddle ponies to the riverbank one day with Addie straddling the seat in front of Leah and me coaxing her to race Taffy up to Harrow Road. "I'd leave you in my dust"—she laughed—"if I wasn't hanging on to Addie."

"Where did you learn to ride?" I asked her when we'd slowed to a walk. The prairie spread out before us like a green ocean. "You sit a horse just right, as Pa says, even in your skirts, lookin' like you were born in a saddle."

"I learned bareback first," said Leah. "After that, a saddle's easy."

I looked wistfully at the horizon, not wanting the moment to end. The blue dome of the sky arched over us and dropped to meet the wheat fields in the distance as if a painter's brush had drawn the edge. "It looks like you could gallop right up to heaven if you rode far enough," I said, "and maybe meet the angels there."

Leah caught hold of my mood. "That's what I'll do someday when I take off to Zion. The folks there are actually called saints, you know."

I looked across the lush green pasture. Wild flowers were blooming in the prairie grass. "I don't know why you'd ever want to leave our Kansas countryside," I said. "Unless it was to get away from Quantrill and his Bushwhackers. But if it's him you're scared of, you don't have to worry. We've got lots of protection here in Lawrence."

"Where is Leah going?" Addie wondered, adding her usual sentence to the conversation. We laughed, and Leah lovingly squeezed Addie.

"I'm not too worried about Quantrill." She took up the thought as the horses began moving again. "He's not why I'd be leaving."

"Then I don't see why you'd ever want to go. Addie loves you, you know. It would be like losing her mother all over again if you were to disappear."

Leah looked across the horse's mane, a little surprised at the remark. Then she stared at me thoughtfully.

"You're always talking about Zion and how you're going there," I pouted. "Why can't you just stay here?"

She waited until I raised my eyes to hers, and then she reached across the saddle to touch my hand as I held my bridle. "I'm not going anywhere, Ethan," she said gently, "not right away."

I felt better after that and enjoyed the ride. I remember looking around the fields and trees we passed and wondering if Rand Saugus was nearby. *I think I've seen her*, he had said. *She has dark hair and rides the buckskin pony.* Well, let him look, I thought. No one would bother Leah while I was around.

★

I don't know exactly when it was that summer that my feelings toward Leah began to change. There's no one moment when a young fellow suddenly grows up. I only remember that, for me, friendship and innocent adoration became something more, something that aroused jealousy, pain, the urge to protect, and a dozen other emotions I couldn't explain. It was a different kind of attraction I had never grappled with before. Leah had always been beautiful. I guess "pretty" is the way a fourteen-year-old boy would have said it. But, early on, that just meant she was pleasant to have around, like a lovely painting or some rich, eye-catching design. You're attracted by the art, but you have no real emotion for the object. Then things change. You change. And when you're a kid, you don't really know why, and you can't put your finger on the time or place that a special warmth comes stirring in your blood.

Maybe it was the day I was in the upstairs hallway and had an urge to go into my mother's room. Leah saw me from the landing, first watching as I hesitated and then coming forward to gently encourage me to walk through the door. "I know you see this room as dark and sad, Ethan," she said, "the room where your mother died, but it's all right to come here, to remember that it's a sacred place as well."

I stood like a statue in the doorway as she drew the curtains back and let the sunlight in. For the first time in almost a year, my mother's room was no longer cast in shadow. Her bed was there, neatly made and never slept in since Mr. Tellis, the mortician, had taken her away amidst the wailing of friends on that gray, drizzling morning when she passed. Mrs. Kreiger had cleaned and freshened the room from time to time, but for the rest of us, it was emotionally off limits, and I had always kept my distance. Even Pa slept downstairs when he was home and never ventured near the room, as if it were a shrine where only angels came to tread.

"You should feel free to come here, Ethan." Leah's hand was pressing on my shoulder. "I think your ma would want you to. You know, our loved ones who have passed really aren't that far away. Sometimes their essence lingers in places they've been. I think we honor them by seeking out those places from time to time."

She guided me into the room, and together we looked at the varnished bedposts and the dresser and the side lamps, which had been dark so long. At the bottom of her bed, my mother had a large cedar chest and an apple-red knitted shawl folded over it that I nearly wept to see again. I lifted the shawl and held it close while I stared at the chest, hesitating. It had been a long time since I'd sat on the floor with my legs curled under me, watching with delight as my mother drew her treasures from the chest and laughed with me and Addie over her "prized possessions"—jewelry, dishes, keepsakes, old photographs in silver frames.

Leah seemed to read my mind. "Don't you suppose she'd want you to remember her here?" she said gently. "Don't you think she'd want you to cherish the things she treasured? This is where her soul is, Ethan. It's all right for you to visit here from time to time and feel a piece of it."

Bending down, I carefully raised the lid of the cedar trunk, and Leah knelt with me to peer inside. The faint but lovely odor of cedar-wood and the rose-petal packets on top of the linens filled the air.

"Oh, smell how fresh it is," said Leah, taking in the fragrance. "It's your ma's perfume, you know, these lovely scents that float here still."

"Can it be like that?" I suddenly asked her. "Can she still be here through these things of hers that we touch and hold and see and smell?"

"Certainly she can." Leah's round eyes brimmed with tears, and she placed both her hands on my shoulders. "Our loved ones remain with us forever in memory, and often it's the tangible keepsakes—the things we can see and touch—that keep the memories fresh."

I looked into the box and drew out an ivory pendant on a golden chain. It was elegant and simple, a lovely oval edged in gold. I held it in my palm and let a sliver of its chain slip through my fingers. My mother had often worn this piece. "I remember this," I said, running my thumb along its face.

"It's lovely," agreed Leah.

A wave of emotion suddenly flooded through me, and before I could stop myself, I turned pleadingly to the young woman at my side. "I want you to have this. Please take it. Wear it as my mother did, to remind me of her."

Surprised, Leah hesitated. "Oh, Ethan, are you sure . . . ?"

"Please take it. When you wear it, I'll remember her."

She relented with a soft smile and took the pendant in her hands. "I'd be honored." She carefully placed the chain around her neck, adjusting the clasp so the ivory oval fell perfectly below her collar. "It is beautiful," she said, still fingering the pendant. "I'll treasure it, Ethan, and wear it during special times. Thank you for trusting me with such a gift."

Yes, maybe it was then that I started seeing Leah differently that day in my mother's bedroom when the ivory pendant first hung around her neck. She looked lovely wearing it, lovely in a different way than I had anticipated. Soon it wasn't my mother I remembered when I thought of the ivory oval as much as it was Leah, her graceful movement, the way she warmed a room, the way her eyes glowed when she smiled.

The day I gave Leah the pendant, I also showed her my mother's closet where some of her dresses still hung. I offered them to Leah if she ever wished to wear them, and she graciously accepted, saying, as with the pendant, that she'd be honored. I couldn't believe the feeling that came over me the first time she actually donned a familiar tunic of my mother's. It was as if affection and beauty had returned to our lives and to our home.

Certain feelings sometimes creep up on a boy, even before he's yet a man, and I suppose that's what was happening to me. In the springtime you're an awkward kid, all bones and angles. By autumn you've filled out, sturdy and in your prime. I didn't sprout physically that summer. I was still fourteen, but I began to change *inside* a little, and that shifting aspect could be gauged, I guess, by what happened one warm night when Bobbie and Toe-Jam decided to sleep over. That incredible night when my initiation was complete.

We were on the lawn at first, me and Bobbie and Toe-Jam. We'd spread out blankets and planned to map out the constellations once darkness fell. Mrs. Kreiger and Leah had cooked up a mess of beans and bacon, and we'd made ice cream out by the pump house, where the ice was handy. Old George had come around to help us turn the handle and stayed to get a bite of what he called "cold puddin'" while Leah led us in a song. "Cracker Joe" was the name of it, and it had a bounce that I could pick out on the guitar once I got in rhythm. I strummed gently, though, because Leah's voice sent a warm thrill through my heart. It was a summer evening made for bees and fireflies and lying in the grass, the kind of evening when you see the first stars come out and you think your youth will last forever.

"You're sure your mother knows you're going to stay all night?" Leah asked Bobbie as she and Mrs. Kreiger cleared up the dishes and old George began to look for his crumpled hat. "And what about you, Henry? Does your ma know where you are?"

"Yes, ma'am," said Toe-Jam. "My ma don't let me go anyplace at night 'less I'm already there."

We all laughed at his bent logic, and Bobbie gave him a playful shove before bowing gallantly to Leah. "We thank you for the supper, miss, and the velvet grass to lay our heads on. We hope you have a soft place to gently sleep as well."

Leah pointed to her window on the second floor and answered merrily, "I'll be keeping an eye on you from my tower perch tonight. So don't you three be running off to scare the neighbors!"

"I'll send George after 'em with a buggy whip if I hear 'em cross our fence," Mrs. Kreiger offered, tromping between us to retrieve the ice cream bucket. For once, I believed Mrs. Kreiger's threat.

We did sneak around a bit after George had meandered off on his old horse to the nearest grog shop and Mrs. Kreiger had gone home. I knew Leah was putting Addie to bed and wouldn't care if we climbed the lattice to the first pitch and gully of the roof or if we crawled through the window, playing Blind Burglar when the lights went out. Leah knew our games, and unlike Mrs. Kreiger, she accommodated them. Like Bobbie said, Leah was a kid at heart.

The idea of Blind Burglar was for all the players to root around the house in the dark until they each found some treasure, something small that could be carried through the upstairs window, across the roof, and down the lattice because that was the designated escape route. If that was impossible or anything was broken or you got caught, your "stealing" didn't count. The fellow who got outside with the best treasure won the game, the bragging rights, and a lot of praise and friendly punches from the others.

Because I had a decided advantage, being familiar with my own house even in the dark, it was stipulated that I must bring my prize from the parlor or the kitchen, which were both downstairs and on the opposite side of the residence. Toe-Jam and Bobbie were free to search the vacant bedrooms of the upper hallway where we entered. This included my mother's long-deserted suite, but I wasn't worried about Toe-Jam or Bobbie stirring through my mother's jewels or her personal belongings. They knew my mother's room was empty and unlived in. My own room was a more likely place to search. It was there on the second floor and down the hall, filled with all those flags and bullet fragments my father had brought me from the battlefield. Luckily for me, most of those things would be hard to find in the dark. I knew there were better treasures in the kitchen. Addie's room, along with Leah's next to the master, were in the hallway too, but as "burglars" we were bent on being stealthy. Being caught by Leah or Addie would only spoil the game.

It was a romp from beginning to end. Feeling an appropriate thrill of anxiety, we climbed the lattice and slid on our bellies through the narrow window, one by one entering the quiet corridor that led from the slanted ceiling. I made a beeline for the stairway at the far end of the hall, observing, as I passed her door, that Leah had finished with Addie and was now in her own room, probably reading, as her lamp sent a crease of yellow light under the closed door. All the better, I thought. If she had still been with Addie, chances were good that she'd see as she retired to her room and, at the very least, delay the game. Now both she and Addie were "in" for the night. If we were stealthy enough, we could avoid detection.

I hurried downstairs through the darkness with little trouble. The shadows were familiar, and the moon and stars cast a glow through the lace curtains and above the cornices of the front windows. I already had my "treasure" in mind. My father's gold pocket watch on the mantle in the parlor would not be hard to find. It was a gift to him from my mother, and he refused to take it to battle, fearing its loss.

Quickly finding the watch, I paused, thinking of the priest's hole right there in front of me. Then I retraced my steps to the upper floor and the long hallway to the window above the lattice. Toe-Jam appeared suddenly from one of the empty rooms, and we nearly collided as we both lunged toward the window, suppressing our giggles as we tried to squeeze through. The yellow crease under Leah's door provided some light, but Bobbie was nowhere to be seen.

Toe-Jam and I had both crawled down the lattice and were comparing our "loot" beside the lantern on the porch when Bobbie rounded the corner of the back porch, already down before us and smugly tossing a shiny gold medallion that I recognized as coming from a jewel box of my mother's. "Hey, where'd you find that? My ma's trinkets were put away."

Bobbie looked proudly at the medal and then winked as he tossed it in the air again. "It was on a shelf in your ma's closet in a box shoved back against the wall. I figured it'd be the winner, 'specially since I could get out so quick."

"I woulda beat ya if I hadn't hit Ethan in the hall," complained Toe-Jam, showing off the Confederate battle patch he'd found in the trunk in my bedroom. "This here's a honey of a patch—if I coulda beat ya to the window."

"Ain't nothin' like this medal," said Bobbie, still juggling the piece in his hand. "Besides, I got out first."

I was a little peeved at Bobbie, mostly for mastering a game I had counted on winning, but also for using my mother's precious keepsakes to do it. It was my own fault. I regretted not officially making her room off limits. I would have, had I known there was anything of value in the closet.

The loss of the game and the feeling that Ma's privacy had somehow been violated made me sulky even when Toe-Jam got all giggly over his own success. "I still think I got the top piece." He laughed. "This patch is a bully of a prize!" I told him he could have the patch as his own, and he squeaked like a kid on Christmas morning. "I got a cap at home for my ma to sew this patch on," he cried, slapping his forehead. "Everyone will see I put one over on the Rebels, grabbing their own battle patch."

Toe-Jam and Bobbie both looked with admiration at the pocket watch I'd brought, and that made me feel better about losing the game. They stared wide-eyed at the gold lid of the watch and liked seeing it flip up to show the face. "If I'd known that was on your mantelpiece," Bobbie allowed, "I'd have gone straight for it."

Later, when the three of us had crawled into our quilts on the grass to watch the stars, I let my irritation go, proud in the end that some trinket of my mother's would seem valuable to Bobbie. I waited until Toe-Jam was asleep, and then I asked Bobbie how he found the jewel box in the closet. "It must have been dark as pitch in there," I said. "How'd you see anything at all?"

"Well, I had a little help," he admitted. "Your ma's closet butts up against the wall of Leah's room, ya know. There was a crease of light running a little ways down the split between the boards, right where one of 'em comes up against the corner. It's just worn away enough to cast a pinch of glimmer if the lamp's lit on the other side. It was enough to let me root around a bit and find the box."

"So that's how you did it."

"You didn't say we couldn't use whatever light was there," he reminded me. "I'll bet the moon helped you a little."

I nodded silently. I wasn't worried about the game rules anymore. "Was Leah there? Could you see her through the crease?"

"Sure," said Bobbie indifferently. "I mean, I could see her just a little when she happened to pass by, enough to know she was there anyway. She was moving around, tidying up or something. I didn't want her to hear me, so I didn't look too long."

"Maybe you shouldn't have looked at all."

Bobbie pretended to be insulted. "Well, I ain't no peeper if that's what you mean! I save my spyin' for Quantrill and his Bushwhackers if it's all the same to you!" He rolled over on his back and looked at the stars. "No," he said, "it felt queer enough just being in your mama's closet, Ethan. It was kind of creepy, ya know, your ma being gone and all. I hope you'll return the medallion nice and proper so your ma's ghost won't haunt me over it." He hesitated, pointing his boyish chin toward the stars. "Maybe we should keep our games outside, especially in the summer," he finally added. "Houses and parlor games are more for girls anyhow." He reached over and laid my mother's medallion on my pillow, and I clutched it for a moment before slipping it underneath the quilt until morning.

I felt a weight of regret that left me restless all that night. My dead mother's bedroom should have been off limits in our game. I'd thoughtlessly allowed Bobbie to violate the privacy of her possessions, and even he felt queer about it. An urgency gnawed at me to replace the medallion as soon as possible and make up for my lapse in judgment by locking the closet.

But the next day when I went to my mother's room, I realized it was something besides returning the medallion "nice and proper" that drew me there, and I was ashamed to think about it long enough to let the guilt set in.

Except for Mrs. Kreiger puttering in the downstairs kitchen, our entire house was empty that morning. Leah had taken Addie to a children's frolic in town, and I had been charged with gathering the bedding from the lawn and cleaning up any sign of our ramble through the yard and porches. After that, I was on my own, and I made the most of it. I put the medallion back on the shelf in Mama's closet and then searched curiously for the crease on the edge of the wall that Bobbie had described. It was hard to see until I closed the closet door, leaving the space pitch black, except for a tiny vertical hole that filtered in a sliver of light from Leah's room, made sunny by her open windows. Kneeling down in the darkness, I squinted through the hole and let my eye rove about the room, taking in as much as possible. The hole was small, but I could easily recognize Leah's bed and dressing table, where she undoubtedly sat at night combing out her braid and brushing her long hair. I imagined her there, doing that and whatever else girls do in front of mirrors before they go to bed. I felt a surge of wonder about the beauty of it all.

That night, when it was dark and Addie had been put to bed, I crept down the hallway toward Mama's empty suite. I was a stupid, adolescent boy, more curious than malicious, but still aware of the lines of propriety and suddenly too willing to cross them. The crease of light under Leah's door as I passed it in the hall told me she was still awake, and I tip-toed silently, hoping to reach my mother's closet before Leah's lamp went out.

At the back wall's edge, the pinhole sent a spiral of light into the darkened closet, just as I expected. Carefully, so as not to make a sound, I pressed my eye against that hole again and glimpsed the part of Leah's room that I had seen that morning. This time, the glow of amber from the lamp lent a warm tone to the space as if it were a painting or a sepia-colored photograph. There was motion in the room. Leah was walking about, only slightly visible at any given moment.

Once, as she passed close by, I jerked away, thinking she'd certainly become aware of me. But she hadn't. She was completely caught up in whatever she was doing. I soon breathed easily and silently again. She was humming a tune, I remember, contented in her solitude. I wondered what she'd think if she knew that I was there, just watching in the darkness. I thought about backing away and giving Leah her privacy. In fact, at one point, I shamefully determined to do just that, but I had settled into an awkward position, and any movement would surely give me away. My panic over remaining undiscovered was more violent than my shame, so I decided to follow my original course and satisfy a curiosity I could not explain.

I must have waited several minutes before the moment came. Leah sat at the dressing table and began combing out her long, dark braid. My line of vision was mostly from the back, but I could see her face in the mirror, a reflection softened by shadows and the dimming lamp. Leah's large brown eyes seemed to dance in the shine of the glass. Her features took on a more natural hue, but a blush of color still set off her summer cheeks. I could have watched her all night long, smiling quietly in the mirror, brushing that glossy hair. It would have been a harmless vision with only innocent intent, but at that moment Leah rose up and moved toward a chest of drawers. When she returned, a nightgown hung across her arm, and she was working to unfasten her cuff and collar buttons.

Suddenly, I was so filled with shame that I backed up in the closet with a jerk, pulling violently away from the crease of light. In a panic I stared at the peephole, hating myself for what I'd done and what I'd seen. Desperately I turned to leave, searching in the dark for the closet door. Then I paused, my hand on the knob, and worked to calm myself before I opened it. It was a crucial hesitation. Before I knew it, I had edged toward the light again and risked one last view of Leah, a view I never allowed myself to take. Instead, I clenched my fists and shut my eyes and held my breath until I could finally move without her hearing me.

Strangely, I had experienced a new emotion watching Leah there. It was inextricably coupled with my shame. I recognized how vulnerable this girl was, in her tenderness and beauty, and I vowed at that moment to protect her from every danger that should come her way. I was only an awkward teenaged boy who'd let his curiosity get the best of him. But the urge to protect Leah, to guard and shield her, became a part of every waking hour. She had been a frozen, weeping child in Nauvoo, a castaway from Sarah Willard's door. Lonnie Hodge had sworn at her and called her a dirty Mormon. And now I had acted worst of all, trespassing on her privacy like some miscreant. Was I any better than Rand Saugus, who apparently leered at Leah while he was hiding in the trees? The next morning I got a trowel of cement calk from the barn and carefully sealed the crease hole in the closet. My Leah would be safe. No one would ever spy on her again.

Part Two

Corporal Crockett

Chapter One

It was in July, when Leah attended a dance with us at Colby's Barn, that the colors of my balmy summer began to fade before my eyes. I had looked forward eagerly to our Independence Day celebration, which always included fireworks, a parade down Massachusetts Street, and a community picnic on the town square. Some of the neighboring villages had cut back on their usual revelry this year, especially those who had felt the sting of Quantrill's whip. Civilian gatherings invited lurking Bushwhackers to loot outlying farms or supply stations left lightly guarded. Lawrence was mostly unruffled by those possibilities. "We'll turn our nose up to Quantrill and go on about our celebrating," declared Mayor Collamore, and that was the general attitude. "The war needs our fiery Fourth in honor of Mr. Lincoln and the troops!"

Bobbie, Toe-Jam, and I entered every contest that afternoon—from pie eating to bull-frog racing—and probably won or placed in all of them between the three of us. The picnic featured a fat sow skewered on a spit and turned for hours until the pork was tender and the succulent juices flowed into the fire, casting an aroma that made our mouths water as we lined up with our plates. Salads and vegetable dishes were scattered across a long table. Beyond that was Clem Ford's cider stand, complete with his own make of a strong, fermented brew that drew George Kreiger and several other eager customers. We boys settled for the cider and got a laugh or two out of watching old George try to walk a straight line once his second mug was empty.

The dance at Colby's was the traditional culmination of the day, and it drew families from all the outlying areas, anxious to step spritely as old Mack Appledeen and his Rounders played their fiddles and guitars. They had a bass as well and a drum to set the beat. Appledeen stomped up a frenzy on Colby's hard dirt floor. A brass band had marched in the parade, but the Rounders' skills were made for dancing, and everyone soon caught the spirit.

The ladies came in ruffles and lace and bell skirts that reached their shoes, with their hair curled in ringlets or chignons, large rolls shaped stylishly and netted at the back like my mother used to do. These Kansas girls weren't as fancy as the plantation belles or the Eastern debutantes, I suppose. Their dresses were last year's style and something on the faded side. The war had turned the whole world a little gray, it seemed. But it was the Fourth of July, and Lawrence still knew how to throw a party. The ladies' faces were fresh with smiles and blushes, and I could tell they were anxious to show off their ribbons and their dancing steps, especially the unmarried girls, who seemed more inclined to giggle and nervously spring about from corner to corner eyeing every available man. Leah wore my mother's lacy tunic along with the silver earbobs and ivory pendant I had given her. I thought she looked just swell. I should have guessed that every other fellow would feel the same.

The recruiting office in Lawrence not only gave us safety from Quantrill, but it was catnip for the ladies, drawing a stream of young roustabouts from a wide swath of Kansas, as it did. This summer night several of the fresh, clean-shaven enlistees had shown up at Colby's, all shiny in their spit-and-polish boots and new uniforms. More interested in the sword and pistol an officer might carry, I paid these weaponless recruits little attention. What did I care if these fellows came to dance? The giggly girls could have them. I was thoroughly content to bounce Addie on my knee, watch her clap her hands to the music, and know that nearby, Leah Donaldson was happily conversing with her friends, Juliette Freeman and Mary Carpenter, who were minding the punch bowl at one end of the hall.

It pleased me to see that Leah was becoming a familiar face in Lawrence, with social connections and an avid interest in our town. Her friendship with the Carpenters helped make her entirely acceptable to almost everyone. The old bitty Sarah Willard still turned her nose up whenever she saw Leah and chewed about the "strange religion" to anyone who would listen, but most folks paid her little mind. Leah was friendly and full of life in any crowd. I figured strong friendships might help her forget that mysterious longing for Zion she often spoke of. I liked the fact that she was merry and popular among the women—Sarah Willard notwithstanding—and that Lawrence had welcomed her with open arms.

But that night at Colby's everything changed. I don't know why I didn't see it coming. Maybe I had the mistaken idea that Mormons didn't dance or flirt or court as other people did. Maybe I thought Leah had come to Colby's for Addie and me with no interest in actually stepping spritely like everybody else. Early on, Leah wasn't particularly forward when it came to joining the dancers on the floor. She seemed happy to mingle with her friends and to see that Addie was well cared for. Judge Carpenter graciously danced with her once, before whirling his wife away for all the reels and waltzes, leaving Leah to work the serving table. But if I thought she'd be content to chat with Juliette Freeman at the punch bowl the entire evening, I was due a lesson, and a very hard one.

Corporal Joby Crockett had no sword or pistol. He was one of the fresh recruits who paraded out in front of Lawrence's female population to be fawned over and honored before going off to war. It was the army's reward, I guess, to these boys who were as naive as I was about the reality of battle. "Become a brave and dashing boy in blue," was the recruiter's siren call. "See how the pretty local girls will flock around." The idea was surely behind many a prompting at the mustering station where green lads from across the eastern counties came to enlist. "These girls are eager to appreciate you, to send you into battle remembering their soft cheeks, their perfume, and their kisses. Sign on, before the other fellows skim the cream!"

Now that I'm older and know the way of things, I'm slower to cast blame and judgment. War collapses time, driving folks to alter their priorities. Boys filled with bravado are often also filled with fear, an anxiety that pushes them to fall in love too fast and for misguided reasons. Every girl who's attracted to a handsome soldier is faced with a dilemma. He is young and going off to serve his country, perhaps never to return, with so few of life's joys realized. Many girls were willing to reward such honorable sacrifice with somewhat dishonorable behavior, excusing the action as a "gift" owed to the brave and valiant boy who might never come home again. At thirty years old, I understand. At fourteen, I hated Joby Crockett from the moment he first appeared at Colby's and asked Leah Donaldson to dance.

He was tall and broad shouldered, with thick dark hair across his brow, and a ready smile on his lips. I suppose the women thought him handsome, though without the bars and buttons of an officer, he looked quite ordinary to me. His uniform was plain and unadorned. There was no bluster about him. His eyes were dark, I remember, and never left Leah's upturned face while the two of them were dancing, which was every round once he'd first reached out to her from across the serving table. "May I have this next dance, ma'am?" he'd inquired courteously, choosing Leah from among four other women standing there and surprising her with the effort he made to draw her out. I saw it all. Crockett was so polite and polished that he cast a spell on Leah. He led her from behind the table, displaying perfect grace as they merged into the throng of dancers. They seemed a perfect couple, and all the others turned their eyes to see. Leah was a beauty, moving in her common frills and lace, and from then on Crockett never left her side. They shared every waltz and polka, sweeping gracefully among the other dancers, floating on a cloud. They laughed and sang together during the choruses as if they'd practiced many times before—"The Union Forever," "Yankee Rag," and "Liberty at the Gate." During the intermission they drank punch and ate a slice of cake off the same plate, merely nibbling at the crumbs because they couldn't take their eyes off one another.

I watched all of this, squeezing Addie's hand and burning with a jealousy I never knew I owned. I couldn't understand why Leah seemed so smitten with this fellow. He was more poised and self-assured than some of the other fresh recruits who brought their scuffed boots and backwoods slang with them, as awkward as cattle in a clearing house. I couldn't imagine Leah ever giving any of them the time of day. Crockett stood out, I suppose, as well mannered as he was. He probably smelled of pomade oil, though I never got close enough to tell. Leah certainly did, tweaking his cheek once when he apparently said something funny and dancing well within arm's length as they glided across the floor.

I didn't understand at the time exactly why I hated Joby Crockett. Maybe it was because Bobbie punched me in the ribs as we watched, and teased, "Hey, Ethan, some soldier's got our girl!"

I pushed him back with an indifferent shrug. "What do I care?"

Bobbie whispered maliciously in my ear, "It's good for us, you know. Leah won't give a hoot what we're doin' from now on. Look at her. She's been devil struck. Her every waking thought will be on this soldier fella. You can bet on that."

"How do you know so much?"

"My pa told me how it is with women once they fall in love. They get a gleam in their eyes and a bloom in their cheeks that they never had before. You can see it now in Leah's face, just like Pap said."

"You're crazy. You don't know anything."

Bobbie had proudly worn his handsome, Yankee-blue uniform to the dance. He looked swell in it with its gold buttons and bars and shoulder braid. Maybe he did know something about girls that I had yet to learn. As my eyes followed Leah moving across the room in Crockett's arms, I wondered if it was his uniform that dazzled her. Who smiled that way at a total stranger? Crockett wasn't even an officer. Weren't Addie and I more important than some off-the-farm recruit?

"We've lost her, Ethan." Bobbie winked before he walked away toward the pie table. "You might as well get used to it."

Addie came up and pulled on me just then, wanting to dance. I took her hands and swept her giggling onto the floor, trying to keep track of Crockett and Leah from the corner of my eye. Leah seemed to have forgotten all about us—me and Addie and everyone else in the room. I relaxed a little, enjoying Addie's laughter and clinging to the hope that whoever Joby Crockett was, he'd soon be gone from Lawrence. Soldiers always went away.

Trouble was, this one wasn't leaving fast enough.

"Corporal Crockett has offered to see us home," said Leah, when the dance had ended and we were gathering to leave. She was beaming, both at me and Addie *and* at the tall, smiling soldier at her side, who greeted us with a friendly nod. "This is Ethan," she told him, her hand on my shoulder, "and pretty Addie—the finest children in all of Lawrence!"

"Well, I'll bet they are!" said Crockett, and his brown eyes flashed amiably when Addie reached up, begging to be lifted. Soon he was jostling her in one arm and carrying the leftover breadbasket in the other as if he was a member of the family. Leah had introduced me proudly and made my chest swell out, but I didn't like being referred to as a child. I was nearly fifteen, and I could have gotten us safely home as well as this soldier who looked at Leah like she was caramel candy on an apple.

Outside Colby's, we walked toward our buggy, and I could sense that Leah enjoyed being seen with Crockett. People passed by and smiled. Judge Carpenter tipped his hat, and his wife, Mary, beamed in our direction. Juliette Freeman and Margaret Fitch came chattering toward us, squeezing Leah's hand and laughing about some girlish secret. I dawdled behind, dragging my feet, not wishing to take up the space next to Leah that suddenly belonged to a stranger. They didn't mind me bringing up the rear, and I felt more comfortable not having to answer Crockett's condescending questions like, "You got a rifle, Ethan?" or "How fast can that pony of yours go with a trap behind him?" I wasn't interested. I preferred to lag behind and avoid the stilted conversation. Leah's dark hair fell down her back and shoulders, and her pretty dress with my mother's tunic was all lace and rosebuds. I liked to watch her even if she did take Crockett's arm and smile up at him every time he spoke.

When we got to the rig, Crockett helped Leah up and placed Addie in her lap. As he came around, he slapped old Monk gently. "Hello, old boy." He let the horse nuzzle his hand, pulling on the bit and giving me time to jump in back. Then he slid his hand along the horse's flanks and climbed into the seat to take the lines and drive us home. I risked a good look at him while he was fawning over Old Monk. He was younger up close than he had looked on the dance floor, not much more than twenty-one or twenty-two, I guessed. I couldn't understand what Leah saw in him.

It was late, and as we moved along the road away from the town lanterns, the Milky Way above us was crusting the ink-black summer sky with light. Leah eagerly showed Addie the spectacle, pointing to the sky and responding with music in her voice when Crockett remarked about the beauty of it all.

"It's a night of a thousand candles," he said, his eyes raised with theirs toward heaven. "It's a good omen. Here we are, still warm from dancing, and we have the stars to guide us home."

I guess he meant to be poetic or romantic or something. I got the feeling Crockett was going to take his sweet time getting back to our house and not because of any constellation. As Old Monk clopped along through the shadows, I sensed that Corporal Crockett wished that Addie and I weren't there, that he could be alone with Leah without the "children" hanging on.

"Can the boy take Addie in while you show me where to put the horse away?" I heard him ask Leah.

I was fuming. We could have certainly unharnessed Old Monk and put her in her stall all by ourselves. I didn't like the thought of Leah being in the stable alone with Joby Crockett. But what could I do?

Leah nodded. "Oh, yes. But how will you get back to town? I never thought . . ."

"Don't worry about that. It's not that far, and I'm used to walking."

"Are you sure you can find the way?"

"There and back, thank goodness! That is, if you'll let me come to call."

"Oh, I hope you will. Please come tomorrow if you can." She turned to me. "Take Addie in. You'll do that, won't you, Ethan? I'll just be a few minutes getting Old Monk put away."

"Yes, ma'am." I jumped out of my seat and lifted Addie down. She put her arms around my neck, and I turned my back toward the buggy as I climbed our front steps. On the porch I turned again, and Addie and I stood watching as Corporal Crockett prodded Old Monk toward the barn. Without Addie on her lap, Leah had moved closer to him, leaning against his shoulder as he drove. They were both laughing softly about something, but the jangling of the harness left no clue as to what it was.

"Where is Leah going?" asked Addie, her wide eyes following the trap.

I didn't answer. I just turned and carried her inside, hot down to my hands with a painful anger I had never felt before. My idyllic country summer ended. The dance at Colby's barn had changed everything.

Chapter Two

WHILE MOST OF JULY'S RECRUITS moved out of Lawrence within a few days, proceeding north to Fort Leavenworth for training, Corporal Joby Crockett remained at the station, assigned to help with the clerical work there. Unlike many of the boys, Crockett could read and write, and those skills made him valuable for record keeping and allowed him to wear a corporal's insignia while other recruits began as privates. He would eventually leave for some far-off battlefield, he told Leah, but for the moment, he was needed behind a desk.

I couldn't believe my misfortune. Crockett wasn't going anywhere, at least not very soon. Leah was delighted by this news, while I could only scoff and mutter petulantly to Bobbie and Toe-Jam about Crockett's annoying presence in our parlor nearly every night. "He takes up all her time," I grumbled. "He ought to be with Grant in Mississippi or somewhere in Pennsylvania mopping up for General Meade."

Just hours after our Fourth of July celebration, word had come of the great Union victory at Gettysburg after three days of bloody fighting that had left both armies decimated. The newspapers put the combined casualty count at more than 50,000 men, and our townspeople shuddered at the thought. A report soon followed that the Fourteenth Kansas had been there in Pennsylvania, battling General Lee, and I wondered anxiously about my father until a letter finally arrived. *I have witnessed the greatest battle ever fought on American soil and come through unscathed*, he wrote. *Long live liberty and freedom!*

While my father and thousands of brave men like him were risking everything in the field, Crockett remained behind a desk in Lawrence—and he often found a comfortable chair in our front parlor once his duty there was done. Leah brightened like a Christmas bauble every time he came to call, and I got used to her nervous efforts at seeing that both our parlor and the people in it were polished before every visit. She always had Addie curled and pressed and wearing a pretty little frock, and she insisted that I present myself with my face clean, my hair slicked down, and my white shirt properly buttoned "for the benefit of company."

"Hello, Ethan!" Crockett always greeted me with a wink and nod. "You and Bob catch anything today?" He was referring to the string of fish we sometimes brought home or the occasional rabbit we brought down with Bobbie's little carbine rifle. I took quick offense. Crockett had caught wind of our "lookout" effort against Quantrill in Detmer's Grove, and from his tone I guessed he was making fun of us. "You boys can sneak about, can't you? Better than us big fellows for finding all kinds of varmints. You got the leisure too, with no captain ridin' on your back. I'd like to do some hunting, but I'm always pressed for time."

He seemed to have plenty of time to court our Leah, and I wanted to tell him so, but I didn't have the nerve. Whenever we were alone for a moment—if Leah was in the kitchen getting lemonade or helping Mrs. Kreiger put the last touches on a Sunday dinner—I would fidget in my chair, wondering what to say.

"Makes me wish I were a kid again," Crockett often mused, "free to roam the prairie with no concern. That's what a boy like you can do, and I envy you for it, Ethan."

Once, he bent toward me on the sofa as if he were about to share a secret. "Of course," he whispered, "being here with Leah makes me happy I've grown up!"

He probably expected me to grin or wink at the remark; I wanted to punch him in the mouth. Leah and Addie floated in with the tray just then, saving us both from further shame. But I knew what Crockett thought. I was a runny-nosed kid who still played games while he was the fancy soldier, fighting for his country and winning Leah's heart.

Once, Crockett joined Bobbie, Toe-Jam, and me for a ramble through the woods on the west side of the river. Bobbie and Toe-Jam liked Crockett. He wore his uniform and paid a lot of attention to their palaver about the fish they caught and the trails they knew.

"Where d'ya hail from?" Toe-Jam asked him. "The bloody part of Kansas that Quantrill is after or the part where twisters ar' yer only worry?"

"I come from down around Emporia, not so far away that we don't have to keep an eye out for Quantrill and his raiders. You're safer here with the recruiting station and the army all around."

I suppose he thought Leah was also safer with a tall, broad-shouldered fellow like himself keeping her company all the time, but I didn't think she was safe. I knew what Crockett was after. Lots of kisses and caresses after midnight and a pretty girl to brag about to his friends in the trenches of some far-off battlefield. No, I didn't think Leah was safe at all, and when Bobbie and Toe-Jam ran ahead to check one of our traps, I tried to state the facts to him.

"Leah is a Mormon girl, you know," I said.

Crockett seemed amused. "She told me. It makes no difference."

"Mormons like to stick together with their own."

He considered this and shrugged. "Well, I don't think there's any other Mormons in Lawrence, so apparently Leah's happy taking up with you and Addie . . . and me."

He was being flippant at my expense, but I pressed on, trying to sound mature. "She's making her way to Utah as soon as my pa comes home. It's what she calls Zion, and nothing or no one will stand in the way of it."

"It might be a while until then. And who knows what'll happen in the meantime? When I'm sitting close to Leah, she seems to like it here. She doesn't seem to be thinking about Zion anyhow. You know what I mean?" He winked again as if Leah's supposed adoration of him was a secret between us fellows.

I bit my tongue to keep from saying what I thought. I wanted to blurt out that I didn't like his tone, that he knew nothing about Leah or any other Mormon woman either. Why, Leah would no more let him kiss and cuddle up to her than George Kreiger would give up drinking, and I knew that for a fact.

"You seem mighty concerned about me and Leah being friends," Crockett observed, passing his switch stick through the grass and looking down at me in a slightly puzzled way. "She got another beau somewhere? A Mormon boy I don't know about?"

I shrugged self-consciously. "Leah has lots of beaux. They come through here all the time on their way home from the war. One's due any hour now if you want to know the truth—a lieutenant from Topeka who writes her every day."

"If he does"—Crockett winked at me again—"the fellow's out of luck. I think she's forgotten all about him. She seems a little partial to me, if you know what I mean."

I still didn't like his cocky attitude, his self-assurance where Leah was concerned. Who was he to think he had the upper hand?

Bobbie and Toe-Jam came running up just then, so any talk of Leah ended, especially when Bobbie told us breathlessly, "There's a stranger comin' up the west side of those trees over yonder, that grove of maples by the river. He's sneakin' along like he's up to no good. Toe-Jam and I came runnin' when we spotted him. Maybe he's one of Quantrill's scouts come to reconnoiter."

"Did he see ya lookin' his way?" asked Crockett casually.

"He didn't see us at all!" I could tell Bobbie was perturbed that Crockett would doubt his skills. "Me and Toe-Jam know how to creep out of sight, and this fellow looked like he needed tracking."

Joby Crockett lifted his rifle, slinging it across his arm. "Let's go see."

While we boys got all feverish with our hearts a-pounding, Crockett seemed mostly amused, following Bobbie and Toe-Jam just to humor them. The cloudless sky was blue above us and the air a stifling simmer. I wondered if the many tales I'd heard about the "heat of battle" were taking hold of me. I wondered what Leah would think if she could see me chasing danger like I was. We tramped across a wheat field toward the river, keeping low and careful as we moved along. We let Crockett take the lead once the west trees came into view, and he seemed to know what he was doing. He kept us behind him, signaling our movements with his hand and staying alert for any sound from up ahead.

A shabby-looking stranger suddenly appeared out of the trees. He was tall and lean and hungry-looking with a bent nose and sallow cheeks. His eyes were hard and empty. We saw no weapon on him.

"You there!" Crockett called, and the man jerked up straight, looking around as though he would run but then changing his mind. We were on him now, and Crockett got right in his face. "What are you doing out here? What are you lookin' for?"

The man eyed our hunting rifles and Crockett's uniform, warily holding his ground. He looked narrowly at Toe-Jam and let a whistle of spit leave the side of his mouth. He rubbed his whiskers with an oily hand.

"I asked you what you're doin' here," repeated Crockett, showing off a little with his tone. "This is private land, you know."

Scowling, the fellow raised his chin. "You let that black kid on it," he said, nodding toward Toe-Jam.

"Who are you, anyway?" Crockett spoke sharply. "You one of Quantrill's boys?"

"I'd be proud to tell ya if I was."

"Quantrill's a cold-blooded killer," Crockett snapped. "I wouldn't be praising his name around here if ya know what's good for you. Folks'll likely take offense."

"Quantrill's a fine soldier, the way I hear it," declared the stranger. "I guess it's all in who's doin' the talkin'."

"Talking's cheap, mister," said Crockett.

The man eyed Crockett's rifle and then gazed sullenly at the rest of us. "I'm just passin' through," he said. "Thought I'd skirt around Lawrence, knowin' it's full of abolitionists. I don't cotton to those slave lovers." He shot another dark glance at Toe-Jam and let the spit fly again.

"Well, seeing as how you ain't armed and not in uniform, we'll let ya go," said Crockett. "If you was a Rebel soldier, I'd have to take ya in."

"He's a spy, come to check out the town!" yelled Bobbie, suddenly on fire. "Ya can't let him go! He just as much as told ya."

"Hold on, now," said Crockett, barring Bobbie with his arm. "We don't know he's a spy. He looks more like a lowlife slacker to me, not worth the cost of a night in jail and the dinner we'd have to feed him." Crockett pawed over the man, searching for a weapon and finding nothing while Bobbie squirmed, still fuming.

"You've got a fiery tongue for a kid," the stranger spit at Bobbie. "Must come from hanging around them colored people."

That was all Bobbie could stand. He dropped his gun to the ground, leaped around Crockett, and began pounding the tall man with his fists. "You Missouri swill! You stinkin' Southern scum! You come sniffin' around Lawrence, we'll sic the army on ya!"

The stranger fended the blows off with his arms and finally pushed Bobbie back into Crockett, who had stepped up to drag the boy away. The other man was no worse off except for a deep scratch on his cheek and a black eye Bobbie gave him. He was more angry than injured.

"You keep that little varmint away from me 'fore I twist his gizzard!"

"Hold on, hold on!" Crockett raised one hand, gripping Bobbie with the other. "You go on about your business, mister. This boy ain't no size to fight ya."

Bobbie jerked and twisted in Crockett's grip. "Let me at 'im! I got the vinegar for it."

Crockett held on to Bobbie and looked at the stranger. "Go on. Get outta here while you still got two legs to walk with. Lawrence folks don't like your kind."

"I won't forget that one," sneered the stranger, wiping the blood from his chin and staring a hole through Bobbie, who glared fearlessly back at him. "He's got a nasty little mouth I'll remember."

"See that you do, and stay away," said Crockett. "Now hightail it, like I told ya."

The stranger shrugged and began to slowly turn, looking back at us a time or two as he moved off through the trees. We watched until he disappeared, Toe-Jam and I tense and silent, Bobbie still full of fire.

"We shoulda hauled him off to the adjutant," Bobbie fussed, "or at least ol' Marshal Banks. I got my licks in though, and I'm glad of it. He was trouble and a Quantrill man, sure as anything."

"He was just a tramp," said Crockett, shouldering his gun. "An ignorant tramp isn't worth skinning your knuckles over, Bob."

"He was a proslaver with hate in his eye for Toe-Jam. Should we just stand by for that?"

"Sometimes backin' away from trouble is the smartest thing to do," answered Crockett. "You're not gonna change that fellow's mind."

"I coulda changed the shape of his nose if you'd given me half a chance."

We all laughed, and I felt a new admiration for Bobbie and his swagger. I wasn't alone. "You needn't tighten up yer fists on my account," Toe-Jam piped up, enjoying the moment. "That fella needed a bath more'n a beatin'. I put no stock in him."

We walked back through the wheat field, the four of us, and I wondered what Leah would think of Joby Crockett saving Bobbie from the ragged stranger. I decided not to tell her. She was already too sweet on Crockett without me making a hero out of him. Besides, she might forbid us to tramp through the west fields after that, and I didn't want a boundary on my freedom. I wondered if Crockett was right about the man. Was he just a tramp with proslavery leanings who didn't have the courage to wear the Rebel uniform? If so, there were plenty like him.

I wondered, too, if Crockett would tell Leah. I guessed he wouldn't. He seemed bent on having fun whenever he came to visit, bringing his big smile and cheerful demeanor. He brought out the shine in Leah too, although she'd always been good-natured. But there was a difference in both of them when they were in our parlor. They laughed and teased and said silly things, and once, Leah stole Crockett's cap, and he chased her all around the house to get it back. Sometimes they rode horses together on the same route Leah and I had taken the previous spring. "Joby raced me to the grove and won by two full lengths," Leah reported enthusiastically while Crockett demurred, claiming Leah had let him win and was actually the better rider.

I watched all this with an adolescent jealousy that made me ache inside. The jealousy turned to utter misery one evening when I came upon George and Greta Kreiger chuckling in bawdy tones at the kitchen table.

"Someone needs to tell the adjutant at the recruiting office to kick that Joby Crockett on down the road," grumbled Greta. "He's gonna get his way with our poor Leah if he hangs about much longer. He'll spoil her, sure as the devil—and I'm not talkin' about the pampering kind of spoil. No sirree!"

George gave her his toothless grin and nodded over his pipe. "You think I need to get the shotgun, Granny?" He giggled foolishly.

"That might be what it takes to save our Leah," answered Greta, jabbing her finger at him playfully.

George laughed at the gesture. "The boy needs a little honey 'fore he goes off to war! Who are we to say he don't?"

"Hah!" cried Greta. "*Honey*, is it? Don't you know, old man, that Leah's bound for Zion and wants to keep herself *pure* to do it." Greta tittered at the notion. "It's likely this Joby don't care about no Zion and will try to get all he can from Leah before he goes off to war. It'll break her heart. She's lovestruck over him, but she prob'ly won't give him everything he wants. Still, a handsome boy like him can be mighty persuasive when a gal is cuddled up against him." Greta pondered over the soup she was stirring. "But I think our Leah loves her Zion more."

I couldn't believe my ears. I almost burst into the room, steaming like a fire pot. I tightened my fists and bit my lip to keep from yelling. George and Greta went on in a coarse and teasing way, using language my ma would have washed my mouth out for, having vulgar fun at Leah's expense, and I didn't like it. But the Kreigers were hired people, old and raw-edged. I went away, leaving them to their stupid notions. Who cared what they thought, anyhow? Still, it took me a while to let it go. Mrs. Kreiger's giggles haunted me and made me miserable.

Chapter Three

THE FIRST WEEK IN AUGUST, Joby Crockett brought news that he was finally being sent to Leavenworth and then to join Macdonald's force in Tennessee. He would leave in ten days. Crockett put on a brave face, but I could see that Leah was grief stricken. She'd hold his hand on the sofa and look into his eyes and say sweet things like, "Oh, Joby, do you really have to go?" and "I'll write you. You know I will." She fussed over him like he was never coming back. She helped Mrs. Kreiger fix his favorite dishes and sat with him for hours on the porch. She spent more time with him in town, taking in every party or social gathering that came along.

Crockett wasn't the only soldier leaving at the middle of the month. An entire troop of new recruits was ready to march away, and as usual, when the numbers were that high, the city council sponsored a farewell dinner for the boys with music afterwards for dancing. Since none of the soldiers had families in Lawrence, the evening fell to the matrons and young women to plan and carry out. Children and teenaged boys were not invited. This was to be a gathering of Lawrence's prominent citizens dressed in their finery with its young women expected to attend, dance, and mingle with the departing boys.

"I'm glad we don't have to go," said Bobbie. "High-ho nights like this turn soldiers into prissy fools."

George Kreiger agreed, leaning back against a bale of hay as we boys jested with him. "Yeah," he chortled with his toothless grin. "These fellas walk tall and straight in their stiff uniforms, but most of 'em have never seen a battle. They're as fresh as spring grass, yet the ladies love 'em. Even little Leah loves one of 'em. As for me, I'll cheer when these fellows come marchin' home with Rebel notches on their belts, not at some slick-as-satin dinner party."

"Leah's going," I told him, trying not to show much interest. We were sitting in the hayloft with Toe-Jam, all of us brooding as we looked out the hinge door at the stars. "Crockett's headin' out, ya know. It might be the last time she sees him."

"He'll be back this way someday," murmured Bobbie. "Pa says that once a pretty gal's left her perfume on a fella, he don't ever forget the scent."

"It could be a long time," I said, somewhat hopefully. "And Leah wants to go to Zion before the war is over."

"She never told you that," snapped Bobbie.

"Yeah, she did."

"She said *after* the war was over. Who's gonna take care of Addie if your pa's still off fightin'?"

George laughed at our banter. "He's got ya there, Ethan. Leah's settled here. Could be she'll stay and wait for this Crockett fella. Women turn to jelly when they's in love. 'Course, Crockett could tag along with her," he added, "to Zion, I mean, once the war is over. But don't you suppose them Mormons have feelings about just who they take? It's a place for the 'chosen,' Leah says."

I was glad when George finally wandered off and left us boys to ourselves. We watched him go, traipsing unsteadily along the pathway to his shack.

Bobbie sat up straight with the light of mischief in his eye. "I got an idea. Come tomorrow night, let's sneak down town to the Eldridge and get a peek at the party. They got the gaslights gleaming. We can haunt the windows from outside without no one ever layin' eyes on us. We'll have fun without dressin' up and puttin' on. Why, I know a place we can crawl in under those high steps below the porch. We could hide there and hear people talkin' as they go in and out. Might even catch a tale or two from folks who don't know they're bein' watched." He grabbed Toe-Jam's shoulders. "How 'bout it? A little canoodlin' might be fun to spy on with the soldiers as eager as they are."

"I'll go along," said Toe-Jam. "Maybe we could sneak some pie out the back door of the kitchen."

They looked at me, expecting I would join them, but I wanted none of their chicanery. It seemed a juvenile thing to do, hiding under a porch to spy on couples as they whispered to each other and walked together arm in arm. Besides, I had no desire to see Leah cozy up to Joby Crockett one last time.

"It's your loss if you don't wanna go." Bobbie shrugged. "I say it'll be a joke we won't forget and our last chance this summer to make a play at foolishness."

I was in no mood for it, and the next night as I watched Leah flit about, smiling at a sour Mrs. Kreiger, who was to be left with Addie, and gleefully dancing me across the parlor, practicing the waltz, it was more than I could stand. I almost told her about Bobbie's plan, but she irked me, eager to see Crockett like she was. In a snit, I decided to keep my mouth shut. Let Bobbie and Toe-Jam hear her purring at Crockett. What did I care? We could laugh about it later while Leah was drying her tears over some silly love letter that Crockett wrote. Yeah, let her go unwarned, I decided, if a soldier who was just a clerk was so darned important.

Leah wore a pretty cotton-white frock—the best she owned—covered with tiny rosebuds on the skirt. Her jewelry was simple and from my mother's collection. The ivory pendant hung on a silver chain around her throat, and bobs like tiny diamonds adorned her ears. It helped soothe my resentment to know Leah was a younger version of my mother in those jewels. She was as beautiful as I had ever seen her. When Crockett arrived in a buggy with the Carpenters and came striding up our steps in a newly pressed blue uniform, Leah's round eyes shone so brightly someone might have mistaken the gleam for tears. Her smile belied that notion. She happily swept Joby Crockett about the house so he could give Mrs. Kreiger his regards, nod to old George Kreiger, and give Addie a twirl before sharing a condescending chat with me.

"How are ya, Ethan?" He laid his hand on my shoulder. "You boys been back to the wheat field since we were there?" He winked and turned his attention immediately to Leah, who needed help with her shawl.

We watched them go, heading out the front door like storybook lovers on their way to the grand ball. I held Addie's hand and stood at the window listening to their voices floating back on the air as Leah exchanged greetings with their friends. Mary and the young judge waved from the buggy. They were perfect chaperones. It wouldn't do for Crockett and Leah to ride to the dinner alone.

"Where is Leah going?" asked Addie at the dinner table as we sat with Mrs. Kreiger in a room too big and a table too long for just the four of us.

"You know where she's going," I answered with prickly impatience. "To the farewell dinner for the troops. It's Crockett's last night here."

"Now, Ethan, you speak nice to your sister," admonished Greta, salting her potatoes. "*Where is Leah going?* Why, those are all the words she knows." She chuckled then in her pursed-lipped way, her round cheeks fat and pink. Looking straight at Addie, she teased, "Our Leah's headed for trouble, that's where she's goin'. But you're too young to know about that, now ain't ya?"

Addie looked on, wide-eyed in puzzled innocence. I wanted to drag her away from the table and from the jaded Mrs. Kreiger. I wanted to rush right out of the house with Addie in my arms. Instead I sat there in misery dawdling over my potatoes.

Later, while Mrs. Kreiger stuffed rag dolls and showed Addie how to sew buttons on for eyes, I moped about, wondering what Bobbie and Toe-Jam were up to. I sat on the porch swing while twilight lengthened into evening, and when darkness finally fell, I could make out the twinkling lanterns and yellow windows dotting Lawrence. I imagined music coming from the Eldridge Hotel hall and sweet girlish voices purring to the men in uniform—one voice more familiar than the rest.

I pondered the idea of sitting in that swing, back in the shadows, until I heard the Carpenter buggy and its horses bringing Leah safely home. It was a fleeting thought. I wasn't going to let anybody see me as a lame, lovesick kid, waiting at the door.

After George Kreiger left and Addie was asleep, I loitered in my upstairs room unwilling to get undressed. My window faced the west side of the house, away from our lane. All I could see, looking out, were the shadows of the tallest trees and the stars above them. Even the lights of the town were out of view from my vantage point. For a while I listened for a carriage or the stomp of horses, but a barking dog somewhere in the distance was all I heard. I wondered about this peaceful summer night, so warm and lovely and yet so close to the precipice of danger. Even that day, in Tennessee and Georgia, battles had raged, good men had died. Cannon smoke swirled on many a meadow, and the thunder of guns still echoed as the wounded were carried away. We were sending our fresh recruits out next week to face the fire that had already left so many maimed and dead. Less than fifty miles from us, in Olathe and in Chester, brutal Southern raiders had looted, burned, and murdered. The terror was not far. Yet, that night, the war within me was more violent than any of those images. I finally drifted off, still thinking of my Leah and of Joby Crockett with his arm across her shoulder dancing at the Eldridge. No other crisis mattered.

I was awakened with a start at the sound of Bobbie's voice outside my window. My lamp had gone out, and it must have been after midnight, although there was no clock in my room. "Hey, Ethan, come on down here," Bobbie whispered as loudly as he could. "Toe-Jam and I got something to show ya."

Looking down across my windowsill, I could see the two of them gazing up at me, Toe-Jam moving nervously about on one foot and Bobbie trying to bounce a pebble off the window frame. "Wake up, Ethan, and sneak on down here," he repeated. "You missed a swell time tonight."

"All right, I'm coming. But keep it quiet, will ya?" I climbed out and down the lattice, just as we had done with the blind burglar game a hundred times before. The boys were there to keep me straight up when I jumped the last few feet, and they pounded me with their friendly fists, happy that I'd joined them.

"What time is it?" I asked. "How come you two are still out this late? Your ma will have a fit, Bobbie, and you know it. Yours too, Toe-Jam. And Leah will be after me if your shoutin' woke her up."

Toe-Jam and Bobbie grinned at each other like they were cats that stole the cream. "My shoutin' isn't gonna wake up Leah," said Bobbie with a smirk. "Leah isn't even here."

"Where is she?"

A pinprick stung my heart. The dinner must have ended. The dancing too. Toe-Jam merely giggled, and Bobbie was in no hurry to tell me any secrets. "You know that old gatepost down under the trees, the one that has the stile next to it?"

"'Course I do."

"Well, just come along with us 'cause that's where we're headed. You won't believe your eyes."

Bobbie took off in a rush, but I pulled him back. "Wait a minute! What were you sayin' about Leah? Is she home or not?"

He didn't answer. He only jerked away, still grinning, and I was obliged to follow with Toe-Jam close behind. Near the wooden fence, all twisted over with green vines, that bounded our back lot on the south, Bobbie slowed down; with his hand he signaled us into a crouch. "Shhhhh." He put his finger to his lips and led us to a familiar place in the middle of the fence where a knothole allowed a clear view to the other side. One of the slats nearby had been torn back, and even in the darkness it was easy to see the white gatepost not fifty feet away. Bobbie slid up to the knothole on his knees and made room for me and Toe-Jam beside him. The grass was soft for kneeling, and we pushed some vines aside before peeking through the slat.

"What's going on?" I whispered, wondering why my heart had suddenly begun to pound. "Why'd you drag me out here?"

"Take a look," said Bobbie while Toe-Jam fought to suppress another giggle. "Joby Crockett and the Carpenters dropped Leah off at your place near an hour ago, but then Crockett circled back and met Leah all alone. We figured you'd like to see 'em kiss good night!"

Dumbstruck, I peeked quickly through the opening in the fence. There, beneath the starlight in her pretty cream-white dress, my Leah stood wrapped in Joby Crockett's arms. Her head was tilted toward Crockett, her cheek pressed against his lips. Before I could turn away, I heard her laugh softly, and I heard him say her name in a pleading tone. Their lips brushed against one another, and then he kissed her eagerly, without gentleness. Leah allowed him to continue, even returning the gesture as if she were enjoying the advance. Stunned as I was, for several seconds I couldn't look away.

Bobbie murmured under his breath, "They been at this for an hour, more or less, a cooing and a cuddling just like that."

"I thought you weren't no peeper," I hissed back at him, moving away from the hole.

"Aw, this ain't the same as that. A good-night kiss beneath the trees? We can tease Leah about it later, once Joby's gone for good." We were crawling through the grass and heading home. I wanted to get as far away from that fence line as I could.

"I ain't never seen no kissin' like that," put in Toe-Jam. "Not out where folks might come walkin' about."

"Or spy where they don't belong," I snapped back at him. My heart was pounding, so scared I was of being heard or seen.

By the time we'd moved far enough to stand up straight, Bobbie was laughing again. "Ol' George told me he'd seen Joby and Leah once out by that old shed on the creek, which is probably where they'll go once they get through here."

"The old shed?" I was stunned. "George saw them there? What did he say?"

"He got all 'winky' on me when I asked what they were doin'. 'None a yer business. Yer still too young to know!' Then he slapped his knee like he does and went to chewin' on his gums. But this here proves what he was sayin'. And I aim to tell 'im what I saw. Ol' George will get a bang out of the story, you can bet on that. Truth is, Ethan, we didn't want to tell you, but Toe-Jam and me have seen Leah and Joby like this before."

I looked dumbfounded at Toe-Jam, whose black eyes were flashing. "Yes, sir!" he grinned.

I turned and grabbed Bobbie by the shirt, jerking him toward me till we were almost nose-to-nose. "You're not telling George a thing! You hear me? Not one blamed thing! You keep this to yourself and whatever else you and Toe-Jam saw, you hear me?"

Bobbie tipped his head back, stupefied. He looked down at my fist gripping at his shirt. "Whoaaa, Ethan," he blurted. "I'm just havin' a little fun. George don't need to know if you're against it. Seems like he's seen enough all ready."

I let him go and made a sharp turn away from both of them, marching back to the house with my teeth clenched and tears stinging my eyes.

"Hey, Ethan," Bobbie called, "we never meant no harm."

I couldn't bear for him and Toe-Jam to see my face, red and miserable as it was. I began to run and lost them just before I reached the garden path that led to our backyard. I slowed down there, hoping my friends wouldn't follow, and eventually made my way around to the front door. I wondered if Crockett and Leah would sit there together in the swing when he finally brought her home. I wondered if they'd kiss each other, right here on our porch, and maybe even do some other things they weren't supposed to do. Well, I wasn't going to hang around and see it.

I went upstairs and checked on Addie, sleeping innocently in her bed. *Poor Addie*, I thought, stroking her pretty angel hair and pausing a moment to listen to her breathe. Addie worshiped Leah, and there my little sister was, dreaming on her pillow. What would she think if she were old enough to know that "darling Leah" wasn't an angel after all? She was tainted, just like every other girl who let a handsome soldier have his way with her.

I must have fallen asleep again, for I had no idea of the time when I woke up wondering whether Leah was safely home. I rose and tiptoed from my bedroom into the hallway, looking for the crease of light beneath her door. All was dark, but I thought I heard voices in the house below, and soon I realized the kitchen lamps were still alight.

I crept downstairs, taking each step as softly as I could, and when I was close enough to the kitchen door, I hid in the shadows behind the corner post. It was Leah's voice I heard, and my heart began to race. She was sobbing, garbling her words in the husky sound of misery. Mrs. Kreiger was there too, and while I couldn't see them, I could tell Leah was searching for some kind of answer from the older woman. "Why, Greta? Why?" she pleaded. "Why would he make that demand of me? Why couldn't he love me in every other way? Why wasn't that enough?"

"I don't think he meant no harm," murmured Greta soothingly. "Like I said, child, he's goin' off to war. Boys like him ain't sure they comin' back."

"Are you saying I should have . . . given him what he wanted? Oh, Greta, heaven knows I wanted the same! I could hardly stop myself! I love him! Surely you've seen how he's driven me to distraction these past weeks and days."

There was a pause, and Greta must have gathered her courage a bit. "To be honest with ya, girl, I figured you'd let the boy have his way before he left, as close as you two were. Most girls would, I think. 'Course, I know you have your Zion to think about. I told George that Crockett might sway ya if it weren't for that."

"It *was* my Zion, Greta." Leah sobbed. "I made a promise to God about getting there, and I won't give it up! I won't!"

"So ya done the right thing, then."

"But Joby is so hurt, and even more than that, he's angry. He said I led him on. He said I shouldn't have let him kiss me if it wasn't serious between us, if we weren't real 'lovers.' I've never seen him so upset. It hurts me so to send him away when I've embarrassed him like this."

"He needs to do the right thing too," replied the worldly old woman, who must have been patting Leah's cheek, for I'd never heard her seem quite so motherly. "Virtue ain't only just for girls, ya know."

"Sometimes it seems that way," whispered Leah. She was quiet then and must have taken a moment to dry her tears. When she spoke again, it was with more clarity. "I should never have let Joby kiss me like he did. I'm at fault, I know. It led him to expect things from me I couldn't give. My virtue is all I have, Greta. It's all I have to offer if God will help me get to Zion. I couldn't give up that dream. I didn't and I won't!"

"'Course not, girl," said Mrs. Kreiger. "I never really thought you would."

★

"Ethan!" Leah's voice at my bedroom door woke me the next morning. "Addie and I are going to the train station to say good-bye to Joby and the rest of the recruits. Do you want to come along?" She knocked softly and then paused, repeating the invitation. "Ethan? Are you awake?" Her tone was full of anticipation, not the misery I'd heard the night before. "Joby would love to see you before he leaves," she pleaded, "and we owe him a good send-off."

You took care of that last night. I murmured the rebuke and hid beneath the covers, remaining silent until Leah went away. I was still angry about what I'd seen in the orchard, even if she'd sobbed to Mrs. Kreiger about not "giving in" to Crockett. To my way of thinking, she'd gone too far, kissing him as she did.

I made my own way to town after I got up. I loitered on the fringes of the crowd at the station as several hundred people sang songs and waved flags, watching as the departing troop of about twenty soldiers marched forward in close rank. Joby Crockett was among them, his chin stiff, his eyes unblinking, his step marking the measure of the drum. The engine whistled and sputtered steam, the bystanders cheered, and when the men broke rank to board, many a citizen stepped forward to shake a soldier's hand and wish him well. Mothers and sisters pressed extra food and clothing upon some of the boys, but most of the troopers came from other places, with no real friends or relatives in Lawrence.

From a distance I caught sight of Leah standing with Addie and telling Crockett good-bye. She was smiling and carrying a flag, which she handed to Addie once Crockett turned to go. With her hand on his arm, she gazed up at him. He bent to give her a quick kiss on the cheek. They spoke one last time, and with a final wave, he walked away, his backpack on his shoulders and a rifle on his arm. He didn't seem so jolly and lighthearted now, and I think he even frowned when Leah tried to press against his shoulder one last time. Leah looked as sad as I'd ever seen her, maybe because of the way Crockett turned his back on her and never looked at her again.

Leah and Addie waited with the rest of the crowd until the train pulled away, sending their smiles and best wishes down the track. I heard the engine and the cheers as the train chugged north, but I was gone by then, walking through the field toward home. I didn't want to run into Bobbie or Toe-Jam or anybody else that morning. Leah may have still been worthy of Zion, but after what I'd seen in the orchard she was no longer who I thought she was. Somehow she was different, though I didn't know exactly why. Breakfast was a sullen affair with Mrs. Kreiger, who didn't like rewarming the mush or skimming off another cup of cream. "Breakfast early, breakfast late," she complained. "And I expect George to show up somewhere in the middle. Ain't seen him yet, though I suspect he's at the station with ever'body else. A noise will draw that man quick as anything."

She eyed me up and down as if she wanted me to say I'd seen George at the depot, but I ignored her, eating my mush in silence.

"Well, ain't you in a mood today!" she railed. "As if I won't have my hands full once Leah comes home cryin' after sendin' that beau of hers off to war." Mrs. Kreiger's voice was not the soothing one I'd heard the night before speaking to Leah. She was back to the strident tone she generally used with me.

"I don't care what Leah does," I told her.

"Now ain't we snippy this morning." Mrs. Kreiger eyed me before returning to her work. "Leah's got a hard spell comin', so you be good to her. That fella Joby had gotten to her heart."

"They seemed kind of angry at each other at the depot, like Leah maybe told him off or something. I don't think she'll cry for him too long."

"Oh, you don't know women, do ya? She'll cry for him all right, for a little while anyhow, till another handsome fella catches her attention."

The images in the orchard flashed before my eyes, and I snapped sarcastically, "Oh no, Leah's a *proper* Mormon girl, and she's going to Zion once the war is over!"

Mrs. Kreiger stopped kneading the bread dough and looked at me, startled by my tone. "What's got into you, Ethan? You ain't never been so snippy when it comes to Leah." She jabbed my shoulder with a doughy finger. "Do I hear a little bit of jealousy in your words? You mad at Leah now because she mighta cozied up to Crockett a little and she ain't the angel on a pedestal you thought she was?"

"That's crazy."

"You got a lot to learn," said Mrs. Kreiger with a jaded grin as she turned back to her baking.

But I wasn't finished being bitter. All this time I had defended Leah in my heart and mind against the Kreigers and their stupid conversations. I'd put up with Bobbie's teasing and silly jokes and with Toe-Jam's eagerness over spying on Leah and Crockett. I had believed with all my soul that they were wrong about Leah, that she was different. Now I wasn't quite so sure, and it angered me that I had ever loved her.

★

My adolescent spite didn't last. In a day or two, I began to sympathize with her. I could see that she was sad and guilty about Joby Crockett and kept to herself a little. For a while she begged off reading to us at night and only toyed with her food at dinnertime. She was careful to be cheerful around Addie and always sent me out the door with a pleasant smile and her usual send-off, "Be my best fellow today, Ethan. Make me proud!"

About ten days after Crockett left came an evening that permanently ended any lingering anger or ambivalence I might have felt regarding Leah. She and Addie were sitting on the porch, dawdling in the swing, and I was leaning against our doorpost watching them and taking in the reverie that summer offered. A languid Kansas sun slipped slowly into the horizon. The August light was fading—as every summer evening should—with a mellow stirring of the air, soft breezes brushing through the high trees, carrying the scent of the roses that flourished near our gate. Crickets had begun to chirp as the sky turned deep blue, and soon we could see the lanterns and gas lamps winking in the windows and on the not-too-distant streets of town. Nearby, our neighbor's wheat looked like the anthem's amber waves. The cornfield next to it was at its prime—green and abundant and waiting to be shucked. Just then, Bobbie and Toe-Jam emerged from the trees across the lawn and moved in our direction. I stood up and waved.

Leah, seeing them, called, "Hello, you two. Come join us."

They came, mounting the steps to our long porch and finding places there, Bobbie sitting against the white rail and Toe-Jam squatting in the corner.

"You boys heading home?" Leah asked as Addie cuddled against her on the swing. "It's getting dark, and your mothers will worry."

"We've been up the ladder at Detmer's Grove," Bobbie told us. "We came down as it was getting darker, and I told Toe-Jam I'd walk with him to Harrow Road before I turn back toward town. Then we saw your porch lights flicker, and we thought we'd stop a minute."

"I'm glad you did," said Leah.

Toe-Jam spoke up, fidgeting a bit as he talked. "You still sad, Miss Leah, 'cause Corporal Crockett's gone away? Things ain't been the same around here since he come, and now it's even worse now that he's left."

A bit startled, Leah looked at Toe-Jam's round eyes and hesitated.

"You need to mind your own business, Toe-Jam," I jumped in. "What do you know about anything?"

"No, it's all right." Leah put up her hand to stop me. "I don't mind. Henry's right, you know. I've been neglecting my best friends."

She slid over in the swing, pulling Addie with her, and I moved to sit with them. It wasn't anything Leah really said or did, but something drew the five of us to lean in closer, to tighten our small circle and laugh at what we had together.

"We got to confess, Miss L," said Bobbie, suddenly dropping his chin. "We're bursting inside, and we'll always get the giggles around you until we let it out."

"What is it?" said Leah cautiously. "A secret?"

Before I could let out a weak alarm, Toe-Jam squeaked merrily, "We seen you kissin' Crockett out by the stile. By Jove, we did!"

Bobbie nodded, laughing. "We sneaked along the slat fence on our bellies. Through the knotholes we could see you real good. And it wasn't just a peck on the cheek you was givin' him neither." A natural teaser, Bobbie couldn't resist watching Leah blush.

"Was you really that much in love, Miss Leah?" Toe-Jam was still laughing guilelessly. They didn't know about Leah's break with Crockett and the reason for it.

"You little rascals!" Leah feigned offense. "I suppose Ethan was with you too. I can't believe it! You three spying on us like that!" She looked at me with a twinkle in her eye, and I shamefully affirmed that I had been a part of the conspiracy. Since I was closest to Leah in the swing, I'm the one that got the playful pummel on the shoulder. "I will never forgive any of you, of course, and I promise someday to pay you back when you're trying to do a little courting of your own."

"Thunder!" cried Bobbie. "You'll never catch me doin' *that*! Besides, *you're* our best girl, Miss L. Ethan thinks he owns ya. But he shares ya a little with me and Toe-Jam, and that's fine with us."

"It's fine with me too!" Leah gestured good-naturedly toward him, forgiving our indiscretions and meeting our foolishness with a familiar smile. I was thrilled to see that Leah was herself again.

"Ethan's always talking about you going away," said Bobbie, leaning against the rail. "'Leah's going to Zion,' he always says. 'Soon as the war's over Leah will be gone.' Is that the truth? Do you figure on headin' out once Mr. Pace comes home?"

Leah hesitated, and Addie popped up from her lap to innocently ask, "Where is Leah going?" It sent us all into gales of laughter at her famous sentence, coming on cue as it did.

Cupping her hands around Addie's cheeks, Leah answered joyously, "I'm not going anywhere, my angel. For the moment, my friends are all right here."

I know Leah still felt a lot of sorrow over Joby Crockett, enraptured as she had been and then having to send him off like she did. I looked at her there on the porch that night and loved her all the more for what she'd done—and for letting the boys tease her about the kisses when she hurt inside. I loved her too for telling Addie that she wasn't leaving even if Utah and Zion still stood at the end of things in Leah's journey.

I've never forgotten that perfect summer night on our wide porch—the shadows settling in, the rich colors of the August all around, and the five of us together like we were. Maybe it was because of what came afterwards, but that moment remains with me like a lovely dream.

Part Three

Terror in the Morning

Chapter One

"Leah, girl! Leah! Everybody! Oh, everybody! All of you get up!"

I was awakened by Greta Kreiger's frantic voice and her heavy tread on the stairs. "Oh, Leah! Leah, get the children quickly! You must save the children!" I rubbed my eyes and squinted toward my window. The daylight seeping through the blind was still pale and ghostlike, with morning not yet full. Slipping out of bed, I tiptoed to the door and listened for any further sounds. Greta was shrieking, and I was still too much asleep to fully comprehend her words. Leah had met her in the hall, and when I peeked out I could see her throwing a robe over her nightgown as Greta cried, "Quantrill! He's here! We're being raided! Oh, dear heaven, it's blood and murder for us all!"

Leah swept Mrs. Kreiger into her room, trying to calm her before she frightened Addie. "Surely, it's not true."

"Come here an' see!" The woman dragged Leah to a window. "Look out at that cornfield yonder! That's where folks are runnin'! They're hidin' in the corn and in the wheat field on the other side. You got to go, Leah! You got to get the kids and run!"

I hurried to pull on my pants and shirt and gather up my boots as I rushed to Leah's room.

"Quantrill's men are killin' all the men and boys," Mrs. Kreiger said, clutching Leah's robe, "especially the prominent ones. Our Ethan's got a target on his back for sure, being Stephen Pace's boy. You know how Quantrill hates abolitionists."

When Leah looked up, I was standing in her doorway and saw her face turn white. She put her finger on Mrs. Kreiger's lips to silence her, but I'd already heard too much. I moved in toward the window, where I stood with them, looking out at a sight I couldn't fathom. Several men and boys—many I knew—were racing frantically into the cornfield and thrashing about amid the stalks. Many were holding up their trousers as they fled; long nightshirts or half-buttoned vests and jackets flapped behind. Occasionally a woman screamed, stumbling along behind her husband or dragging a wailing youngster with her. Men on horseback, three or four from all directions, came chasing after them, rearing up at the edge of the field and firing their guns into the corn. We could hear the raiders' ugly cursing and the cries of anguish as bullets sprayed the field.

"Oh, dear heaven!" cried Leah as her hand flew to her mouth. "Where are our soldiers? Where's the militia?"

Mrs. Kreiger shrugged helplessly. "I don't know, girl. I don't know!" She pointed in the direction of town, in full view from that window. Smoke spiraled from several homes, and dark billows smothered a line of businesses along Massachusetts Street. The center of Lawrence looked like a raging fire pit.

"Hell is rainin' down on us!" Mrs. Kreiger gripped Leah's arm. "Tildy Frost and her girl come by the house on a dead run ten minutes ago," she whispered breathlessly. "They say Quantrill's men have a list of folks for trackin' down. They're not to touch the women. It's the men they're goin' after." She shot a glance at me and then continued, "Boys, too, if they're big enough or if their pa's on the list and can't be found. My George took a gun and went out to check on things once Tildy came through, and now I can't find him. The fool man should have run for cover. I can't go traipsing after him when I'm needed here."

Again, Leah tried to quiet Mrs. Kreiger for my sake, finally hustling her past me into the hallway. I couldn't take my eyes off Leah. Her face was flushed, and her hands shook as she took the housekeeper firmly by the shoulders. "You've got to go find George, no matter where he's gone," Leah ordered. "Don't worry about us. I'll get Ethan and Addie out through the wheat field and up into those trees above the river. You go find George and see that both of you are hidden. For you, that's the most important thing. We can take care of ourselves. Hurry, Greta!"

Mrs. Kreiger's face twisted in agony, but she moved toward the bedroom door, holding back tears with a sodden handkerchief. "I wouldn't leave ya if it weren't for my old man."

I'd never seen Mrs. Kreiger terrorized like this. She paused as she met me in the hallway. "Oh, dear boy,"—she drew me into her arms—"you're growing tall and straight, the image of your father. We won't lose you, Ethan. We'll keep you safe for his sake!"

"Hurry, Greta!" Leah pleaded, sending the woman on her way before I could say anything. She thumped hastily down the stairs, and I turned to Leah with my shoulders stiff and my pride expanding.

"I'm not afraid of Quantrill or any of his lowlife Bushwhackers! My pa would stand 'em off, and I'll do the same."

"Listen to me," said Leah, gripping both my shoulders. "We have more than pride and bravado to think of now. You heard Mrs. Kreiger, and you saw what's going on outside. We've got to keep our wits about us. We have Addie to think about. You go get her up while I get dressed, and we'll head out and hope to make it before the raiders get this far." She spun while I stood there like a dunce, numbed by a fresh panic I didn't recognize. My chest began to burn. I'd never seen Leah so unnerved. "Run!" she cried. "Run, Ethan!"

Jolted out of my trance, I hurried to Addie's bedroom and found her standing by her bed, rubbing her eyes in wonder and confusion, her long nightgown reaching to her feet. Not bothering to dress her, I grabbed the little shoes which sat on the floor and scooped Addie into my arms. "Come on, Ad," I whispered. "We've got to follow Leah on a little race across the field. Everything will be all right."

"Where is Leah going?" asked Addie nervously. Her round eyes sought answers I couldn't give, and she clung to me like a frightened kitten.

In the hallway, we met Leah, who had quickly donned the simplest of dresses and wore no petticoats. She pulled on her slippers while I found a shawl for Addie on the coat hooks.

"We'll go out the back," said Leah, pausing only to give Addie a reassuring kiss. "Don't cry, angel. Ethan and I will keep you safe. But we must take a little walk outside and make no noise."

From the back porch, we scurried to the pump house and rounded the far corner before slowing down. I still cuddled Addie against me and followed Leah's eyes as she tried to determine the safest route. Shrieks and cries pierced the air behind us, and the thud of horses' hooves and rattling of wagon wheels were mingled with the intermittent sound of guns. From the corner of my eye, I could see the clouds of smoke thickening over Lawrence. Pieces of ash and cinder floated in our path.

Suddenly, Leah put out her hand to stop me and drew me down as she fell to her knees. The wheat field twenty yards ahead, our intended destination, was already filled with fugitives, men and women running helter-skelter in a frantic search of safety. Behind them and to our right, several riders were plowing through one end of the acreage, shouting and cursing at the helpless refugees. I saw our neighbor Mr. Higgins shot down as he ran terrified into the field. He struggled through the wheat after he was hit, leaving a trail of matted shocks. Leah gasped and immediately pushed us behind her. I could see her eyes still searching for a safe path through the field until finally she turned decisively. "There's no hope this way. And it's too open to the north. We'll have to go back and hide somewhere in the house. Bring Addie and keep low. We'll be all right."

I followed Leah quickly back the way we'd come, bent over, staying down. Leah's long, dark hair dropped across her shoulders, ungroomed, fresh from the pillow. Its shine reminded me how young she was—just a girl—and our fate was in her hands. The heat of violence around us panicked me, and I almost took off running, but Leah kept me from it. I couldn't leave her.

The sound of gunshots, screams, and curses rained down on us from all sides as we made our way back to the house. Addie, growing heavy in my arms, whimpered and then began to cry, sobbing and shaking uncontrollably. I tightened my grip on her and whispered assurances in her ear, but it took Leah to finally calm her once we made it to the kitchen.

"Listen, Addie," she said soothingly, taking my sister in her arms, "no one's going to hurt you. Ethan and I won't let them. Be brave and hold back the tears. God will help you. I know he will." Addie's cries diminished, and she stared wide-eyed up at us, still trembling but biting her lips to smother away the last of her sobs.

Putting her down, Leah moved deeper into the house, pausing to contemplate each corner. Finally she ordered, "Quickly, Ethan, bring Addie to the parlor."

We followed Leah as she made her way toward our house's largest room and its stone fireplace and mantel. Suddenly I knew what Leah had in mind, and I cringed in disbelief.

"Help me," she said. Together we pushed away the side slab of stone to expose the priest hole behind it. The space was no bigger than a dust bin or a trunk and barely wide enough for one person to lie across its bottom.

"There isn't room!" I cried frantically. "We can't all fit in there."

"No, but you and Addie can, and it's you they're after, Ethan." Leah pushed me toward the hole, as determined as I'd ever seen her. Before I could say anything, she had me hunched down, half lying, half sitting inside the little pit on top of a cushion from our rocking chair. Then she lifted Addie up and placed her on top of me. I put my arms around my little sister as she nestled against my chest, her head just below my chin. It was tight quarters, and I knew that once the rock slab was replaced, we'd be squeezed in all the more.

Leah bent to look at us, and I saw pity in her eyes along with love and fear and courage. I began to tremble violently, and my heart was pounding in my ears. I could feel Addie shiver against me, and I knew she was struggling too.

"Now, you must listen, both of you," said Leah firmly. "Should the raiders come, they'll never find you here. This hiding place will protect you as long as you stay in it and make no sound. You must promise on your mother's name that no matter what you hear or what anybody does or says, you won't so much as whisper until you know it's safe. Do you understand that, Ethan? No matter what you hear!"

I nodded miserably as tears sprung from my eyes.

"Do I have your promise?"

"What about you?" Suddenly I was panic-stricken. I remembered my mother dying in this house.

"Don't worry about me. It's men and boys they want. I'll be all right if you and Addie are safe. That's all that matters."

Leah patted Addie one more time and ran her fingers through the little girl's curls. "Do you make that promise too, Addie?" she asked soothingly. "That you won't cry out or make any noise while Ethan's holding you? I need you to be very still no matter what you hear. Can you do that for me?"

I felt Addie turn rigid in my arms as she answered Leah with a little jerk of her chin. With that, Leah rose and looked gently at us one last time before pushing the slab closed. The stone was heavy, and it took several seconds for her to get it into place, but she called to me once the job was done. "Can you hear me?" she said. "Can you see anything?" Like characters out of Poe, we were prisoners in the wall, engulfed by cobwebbed darkness. But I could hear Leah perfectly, and a tiny sliver of light pierced through on one edge of the stone. "You'll be able to push the slab out when it's over, Ethan. You're stronger than I am, you know."

I knew no such thing.

There we lay, Addie and I, shivering in the darkness, and in seconds, it seemed, I realized we had settled into the priest hole just in time. I heard ugly voices and loud men tromping into the house. I heard windows shatter and lamps crash to the floor. Most of all I heard terrible cursing and an evil tongue I recognized. Lonnie Hodge had come to call—our neighbor, Lonnie Hodge, who skulked about town with misery on his shoulder. He was a full-fledged Quantrill man as we had feared, a Bushwhacker turning against his own hometown.

Greta Kreiger had been right about Quantrill's orders. No woman in Lawrence was to be harmed by the raiders. In an ironic bow to "chivalry" or vigilante "honor," the women would be spared, only to see their sons and husbands massacred. Most of the raiders kept this pledge. While Quantrill himself brazenly ordered breakfast at the Eldridge Hotel, his troops ranged savagely about the town, killing every man they saw, leaving wives and daughters screaming but unmolested in the wake of the butchery.

Leah might have been left alone as well were it not for our history with Lonnie Hodge. Leading a troop of about ten men, Hodge made a point of vandalizing every house along our lane. On our porch he and the others smashed the stylish plate glass windows that framed the entrance and kicked in the oak door, jerking it off its hinges.

With no time and no place to hide, Leah must have stood up straight to face them, for I heard Hodge laugh, "Aw, there she is, boys, standing stiff and tall! Where's your sassy mouth now, Mormon girl? Are you going to push me off yer porch?"

Leah didn't answer him. I felt his footsteps as he stomped toward her. "Where's the boy?" he demanded. "Stephen Pace's kid, where is he?" Hodge's eyes must have surveyed the room. "You've got him hidden, ain't ya? He's somewhere in this house!" Suddenly I heard a loud clap and then another, and I knew that Leah must have felt the sting of Hodge's hand against her cheeks, for she cried out. "You tell me where that kid, Ethan, is, or I'll use a closed fist on ya next!" I heard a muffled squeal that twisted my resolve. Again and again I heard the clap of his hand on her face and cheek.

Addie tightened her grip on my arms. She made no sound, but her wet tears fell on my shirt. I gritted my teeth and clenched my fists and tried to keep from screaming.

I heard dozens of footsteps through the house. They thudded above me on our second floor. "We've searched upstairs and all around," a heavy voice thundered. "We can't find nobody."

"Keep looking," ordered Hodge, and then he must have turned again to Leah. "Where's the little girl? You hid her too, didn't you? Afraid I'd beat the secret out of her? Well, now I'll have to beat it out of you!" I heard the sound of a slap and a groan from Leah. Then he must have taken out a knife, for his next threat sent my hands to Addie's ears. I covered them with both my palms and squeezed my eyes shut against a wave of agony as Leah screamed.

"Ethan Pace!" yelled Hodge. "If you can hear me, you better come on out. I got a blade at this girl's throat, and I'll cut her ear to ear 'less you show yourself! You don't want her blood on yer hands!"

I went rigid and forgot all caution. Were Addie not on top of me, I'd have used my clenched fists to push the stone. As it was, Addie smothered me with her own terror, pressing me so close I couldn't breathe.

"You hear me, boy?" roared Hodge again. "This blade is razor sharp!"

"Hey, Lon," spoke up one of the raiders, "captain's orders not to hurt the women. You best leave this one be."

"Captain's orders, huh?" cried Hodge, cursing. "He tells us what to do while he sits down there at the Eldridge having his ham and eggs?"

"Quantrill's in charge. Best do what he says."

"He said to get the son of Stephen Pace. That's what he said! And I got the list to prove it. I'm warm for the task, I'll tell ya. That kid and his friends always riled me. I'll drill 'im between the eyes and live to laugh about it!"

He must have loosened his grip on Leah, for I heard her rage at him, "You monster! You'd kill a mere boy?!"

"This is war, woman, and that *boy* is big enough to carry a gun! We're soldiers here, determined to take back our rights!"

"You're not soldiers," snapped Leah. "You're cold-blooded murderers. These are civilians you're shooting down!"

"Who are you to talk, you thievin' little Mormon? We ran the likes of you out of Missouri, taking back what was ours, and that's what we're doin' here."

Hodge must have dragged Leah to a window because his voice grew fainter. "See that fella outside, busy tearing down your fence? He's buildin' up the kindling for a fire, and when he gets it going good, he's gonna torch this house! You hear what I'm sayin'? Look out here to the other side. See all that smoke. We're burning Lawrence to the ground, and all them abolitionists and colored-lovers are goin' to be sorry they ever sided with Stephen Pace and old Abe Lincoln!"

Leah's voice was breaking, but her tone was resolute. "Ethan and Addie aren't here, Mr. Hodge. I sent them out across the field before you came. You'll never find them. You're a traitor to this town, Mr. Hodge, and to this neighborhood! All this innocent blood will be on your hands when this day's over!"

Enraged, Hodge let loose on her. "If I'm shedding blood, yours might as well be first!" He must have used the blade again, or tried to, for Leah screamed in terror, and I heard thrashing and gasping near the fireplace. Tears streamed down my warm cheeks; my heart pounded in my ears. All I could do was lie there, hold on tight to Addie, and listen in agony.

"Ho, there! Leave the girl alone! Lay off of her!" Suddenly, a new voice was barking from the direction of our front door. It was

Rand Saugus. I immediately recognized his voice. "Give me that blade, Hodge! What's the idee tryin' to cut this girl? Women are to be spared . . ." Saugus paused and must have put his hand under Leah's chin. "Women are to be spared," he repeated in a gentle tone, "especially lovely ones like this."

"She's hid that Pace boy," argued Lonnie, "Stephen Pace's son, and I aim to put a bullet in his ear before I leave town today."

"What makes you think this girl knows where he is?" Saugus's tone was still controlled, almost pleasant. I imagined his eyes still on Leah as Hodge continued railing.

"Because the little girl's hid too. I reckon they're together. This woman wouldn't let that girl out of her sight 'less she knew where they was. She claims she sent them out across the fields to those woods over yonder, but I don't believe it. They're somewhere in this house, an' I was just usin' my blade to make her tell."

"I believe you're right, Lonnie," muttered Saugus after a moment. He began thumping on the wall. I heard him ask someone if they'd searched the storage hole beneath the stairs and the space under the rafters. On the other side of the stone slab, I was afraid to breathe. I could feel beads of sweat along my forehead, but I was afraid to move a finger. Addie trembled but kept her grip on my arms. For a long moment, it was quiet in the parlor as someone bumped about, examining walls. I could still hear Leah crying softly, but no one spoke.

Then Saugus must have pulled a chair up close to Leah, for his voice returned to its controlled tone as if he were having an extended and genteel conversation, though his feigned courtesy was mocking. "I hope you'll forgive me, ma'am, if I take a seat and converse with you a moment." He paused, probably looking intently at her, for his next words were stunning. "I hope I may be so bold as to tell you you're about the most beautiful woman I've ever seen."

Leah made a disgusted sound but said nothing more.

"We don't get around women much," continued Saugus, "soldiers that we are. Especially with Quantrill. We're always on the fly, you know, runnin' this way and that. It don't give a fellow time for any regular courtin'." Saugus paused again as if to gather his thoughts. "I was married once, and I've known a woman's touch." Again he hesitated. "Some of the fellows have wives or sweethearts waitin' for 'em where we camp. These gals live in caves or little shacks back in Missouri or maybe with their people on some farm. The boys see 'em when they get the chance. I envy those fellas. Soldiering is rough on a fellow's disposition. It's nice to have a woman to come home to, a woman to salve your wounds and keep ya warm at night. I'd like to have me someone such as that."

Again, Leah whimpered but didn't respond.

"Barlow's got that fire built up," Hodge jumped in impatiently. "Let's burn the place and get on out of here."

Saugus ignored him. His focus was on Leah. "I know you better than you think. I've had to sneak around with the Jayhawkers out to get me, but I've had my eye on you. You're a Mormon girl, an orphan with no family, a girl no one will ever try to find."

"I tell ya, Saugus," yelled Lonnie Hodge from the doorway, "Barlow's ready with his torch."

"Please, Mr. Saugus," Leah begged, her voice breaking, "for the love of God, don't burn this house! A dead mother's possessions are in these rooms. It's all they have of her."

Saugus must have stood up then, for I heard him thumping on the wall again. "A mother's possessions? Yes, I reckon so. And I'm not speakin' of photographs and trinkets. A mother's most prized possessions *are* here, now ain't they? I know they are. I don't think you had time to send those kids across the field. You woulda gone with 'em." He banged on the wall with his palm. "They're hidden somewhere in this house, now ain't they?"

"No! They're not here!"

"Well, I'll tell ya," said Saugus, "we're *gonna* burn this house. That's what we came to town to do. You won't give those kids up, but it don't matter. Wherever you got 'em hid, the smoke will seep through and suffocate 'em if the flames don't get 'em first." Saugus changed his tone and seemed to move closer to Leah once again. "You could at least save the little girl by tellin' us where they are. The boy's dead the minute we find him. That's just the way of things in war. But you don't want that poor little girl to suffocate, now do ya?"

Leah was sobbing now. I could hear her panicked breathing. I was ready to push the stone, to scream at Rand Saugus, *Here I am! Leave her alone! Save Addie!*

Then Saugus gave Leah a sickening ultimatum. Speaking deliberately, he said, "I'll tell ya what. You come with me and be my woman like them other fellows have, and I'll spare this house. You ride away with me today on that little buckskin pony I've seen ya with, and I'll tell Barlow to douse his fire." He must have been right up close to Leah, for his words were a raspy whisper I could barely hear.

They unleashed a torrent in Leah, who screamed and sobbed, "No! No! No! No!"

"Now, sweet lady, is it so much that I'm asking? For you to come along nicely and never give me any sass or trouble? That's all I want. Lawrence is in shambles all around ya. But I'll spare the boy and tell Barlow not to torch this house. How's that for a bargain?"

I swallowed hard and strained to hear, but for a moment all that penetrated the stone were soft whimpers from Leah.

"No trouble," Saugus repeated. "If you fight me or try to run away, I'll come back, burn the house, and kill that boy. I swear I will."

"No!" cried Leah one more time.

The sound of Saugus's footsteps moved toward the door. "Tell Barlow to torch the house," he said to Hodge, who must have been happy to oblige.

"Wait!" pleaded Leah through her sobs. "Wait!"

There was a pause.

"Don't burn the house," she said. "I'll go with you. I'll do anything you say."

"With no trouble here or there?" Saugus reaffirmed.

"No trouble," Leah murmured, her voice husky. "Only please, please leave these people and their property unharmed."

"That's my girl," said Saugus, and with a shout he told Hodge and Barlow to put out the kindling fire.

★

I lay behind the stone slab for a long time after the vile noises around our house had ceased. Addie remained on top of me, trembling, whimpering, finally falling asleep. Gripped by fear, I listened for every sound, every possible footstep. At first there were shouts and cursing just outside, then only in the distance—faint but still discernible.

An occasional gunshot cracked the silence, but eventually those, too, were far away and finally gone.

There came a time when I knew the house was empty, our yard and road deserted. I heard our front door swinging on its hinges, and no one was there to close it. Still, I waited. Thinking back, I realize I stayed so long in the priest hole not out of fear of Quantrill and his raiders. The long silence told me we were alone. I stayed hidden out of cowardice. I didn't want to face what I knew awaited me once the slab was pushed away.

Chapter Two

AUGUST 21, 1863—THE DAY WOULD be remembered in the annals of American history as the most brutal attack on a civilian population during the Civil War. The massacre at Lawrence would stain the soul of Kansas, and good people on both sides would look back with shame on what happened there. The carnage was without parallel: 150 men and boys murdered in cold blood, 80 women made widows, 250 children orphaned. Scores of homes and businesses destroyed, a town left reeling, shattered at its heart, wretched in blood and horror.

As we were to learn afterward, the attack had been well planned. From Missouri, William Clarke Quantrill and a column of three hundred men snaked across the border into Kansas, traveling mostly at night and forcing local farmers along the way to guide them. Joined on the road by another troop of 150 Bushwhackers, the army of raiders arrived at dawn on a hill just east of Lawrence. There they paused, some believing the town had surely been warned and was too large and well prepared. Quantrill was of no such mind.

"You can do as you please!" he shouted to his column. "I'm going into Lawrence!" With that, he pulled a revolver from his belt and galloped ahead, yelling, "Kill! Kill! Kill! Lawrence must be cleansed, and the only way to cleanse it is to kill!"

The first man to be shot down was good Reverend Snyder, our pastor from the Briar Street church. He was in his yard milking his cow and was murdered in cold blood as the riders passed his house.

A troop of twenty-two young Union recruits was camped nearby and just waking up. Quantrill's men galloped into the camp, trampling over those still not out of bed and shooting those who were, killing seventeen of the boys before they could escape. The rampage continued as Quantrill's men obeyed his orders to "kill every man big enough to carry a gun." While Quantrill sat down to breakfast at the Eldridge Hotel, his thugs shot every man in sight. Some were shot as they stood at doorways or windows looking out. Others died when the buildings they were hiding in were torched. Prominent men like State Senator Thorp and *State Journal* editor Mr. Trask were coaxed from their homes with promises of protection and then shot once they were on the street. Dr. Griswald, our druggist, was shot with them. Wives screamed and sobbed and begged for mercy.

The raiders went to Mr. Fitch's home and shot him when he came downstairs, firing several rounds into him after he was dead. Mr. Fitch was one of the first school teachers in Lawrence, a kind and respected gentleman. The outlaws torched the house, stopping Mrs. Fitch as she tried desperately to pull her husband's body from the flames.

Two young store clerks, James Perine and James Eldridge, were forced to open the safe where they worked with the promise that their lives would be spared if they did. Instead, they were both murdered after the safe was opened. I knew the boys quite well. They were both just seventeen.

My father's good friend, Amos Willard, the man who admired Leah and brought her to us, was gunned down on his porch, where he stood loading his rifle.

Good Mayor Collamore, knowing he would be targeted because of his position, looked frantically around his home for a place to hide. He and his hired man took refuge in the bottom of a well and cowered there as raiders burned the house. After the raiders had gone and the fire diminished, no sound came from the men in hiding. Mayor Collamore's friend Mr. Lowe hurried down into the well and was killed when the rope broke, sending him to the bottom where the other two men had suffocated.

Leah's friend, young Judge Louis Carpenter, was seriously wounded as he fled from Quantrill's men. Struggling into his cellar, he lay in a pool of blood as the raiders searched the house. They found him soon enough and dragged him into his yard, where they shot him again in front of his young wife. Screaming, Mary threw herself over her husband, shielding him as she begged for mercy. One of the raiders lifted her arm and killed the judge at point-blank range.

George Kreiger was killed, shot down on the street as he headed into town with his old rifle, and Greta was beside herself with grief over a man she'd nagged and scolded for thirty years.

Other victims included Mr. Burt and Mr. Murphy, on Harrow Road, and Mr. Ellis, our German blacksmith, who hid in a cornfield with his child until the raiders found and killed him, leaving the child crying in his arms. Mr. Palmer and Mr. G. H. Sargeant were killed, Mr. Sargeant surviving eleven days with a bullet in his brain.

The brutality could be cruelly random. Some men died for answering their doors. Some were left to watch their houses burn. Still others weren't harmed at all once they were robbed or their families harassed. Some were rounded up, taken prisoner in the Eldridge Hotel, and freed once the raid had ended. Others were immediately shot while trying to surrender.

The Bushwhackers targeted the prominent, burning the finest homes in Lawrence, while leaving the poorer areas mostly untouched. For this reason, colored families generally escaped the butchery. Toe-Jam survived unscathed, as did his father. Their little home, which was small and shabby, looked the same when the raid was over. Of course, everybody suffered, even those who lived to see the sun go down on Lawrence. Every survivor lost someone, a husband, brother, friend, or relative.

History would record that the youngest victim of the massacre was Bobbie Martin, fourteen years old, who was shot down that morning on the path leading to Detmer's Grove, probably mistaken for a soldier in that blue uniform his mother made for him, the one he was so proud of. It numbed me, Bobbie's death, as nothing in my young life ever had. My mother's passing was hard, but it was a natural thing—an illness that finally took her after we all had a chance to say good-bye. Parents often pass before their children do. Bobbie's death was different. He was my age and my good friend. He was me in a blue uniform. I expected to spend a long lifetime tramping the hills with him.

Days later at Bobbie's funeral, Toe-Jam and I spent a long time by the casket. Bobbie lay there in his Union-blue uniform as still as stone, with all the laughter and the eagerness gone out of him, sense-lessly murdered. I thought of Lonnie Hatch's hatred for Bobbie and wondered whether he had sought him out. There was the tramp Joby Crockett had chased out of the field as well. He'd said he would remember Bobbie. There wasn't any way of knowing who had fired the shot. I blamed them all and grimly hated every Southern raider in the war.

"Lawdy, this hurts," sobbed Toe-Jam as we stood there. "I ain't never knew hurt so much as this. That Bobbie was a corker, wasn't he? What we gonna do without 'im, Ethan?"

I didn't know what to say. I just stood there and held on to Toe-Jam, too numb to even weep.

Addie and I survived our ordeal in the priest hole that day, none the worse for being there. I finally began pushing on the rock slab when I heard Greta Kreiger's wails and recognized the voice of Captain Banks, the provost marshal, in the house. Banks helped me slide the rock away, and Addie clamored out into Mrs. Kreiger's arms. I followed, stiff and barely able to move.

Our parlor was in shambles. Lamps were broken, curtains ripped, and furniture upended. The entire house had been ransacked. In the bedrooms, personal possessions were strewn across the floor, linen was torn, pillows tossed, drawers dumped out. My mother's jewelry had been pawed over, and many pieces were missing. In Leah's room it was the same. Books and clothes were scattered about. Leah's dressing table was turned on its top and the mirror smashed.

"At least the house is still standing," Banks said, patting my shoulder, "and you're alive, young man. There's many today in Lawrence not so lucky."

For the next several hours, I remained in a kind of stupor. Even before I learned about George Kreiger, Judge Carpenter, Reverend Snyder, and a dozen other men I knew, even before I learned that Bobbie was dead, anguish flooded through me. Leah Donaldson was gone. My Leah. She had turned herself over to a savage brute to save us, to save *me*. I couldn't keep from trembling. I couldn't stop the waves of panic that overwhelmed me when I tried to speak about it. There was nothing anyone could do.

"Did every rebel get away?" I asked Captain Banks. "Were any captives rescued?"

"I don't know as there was any captives," Banks responded. "And yes, Quantrill and all his men escaped, except one fellow left to take the brunt of things. He's dead now, for all the good it did."

"Rand Saugus took Leah," I told him.

Banks shook his head sadly. "Then I pity her. None of us is in any condition to chase the raiders. We got all we can do right here, those of us that's left. The army will come, I reckon, but Quantrill will be long gone by then, faded back into Missouri and a hundred different hiding places. There's nothing we can do."

He was right. There wasn't anything anyone could do. Leah must have known that when she gave in to Saugus. But she made the bitter sacrifice.

★

Ten days after the massacre, my father returned home, stunned into silence as he surveyed the village and our house. Union officers from Lawrence were allowed furlough to assist their families and their devastated town, and they arrived singly and in small groups as the weeks went by. My father tied Lightning on the fence and limped through our gate, drawing my attention to a serious wound in his right knee that he'd never mentioned in his letters. We met him on the porch, Addie and I, and flung our arms around him as he stared in disbelief at the demolished yard and the smoke-blackened remnants of our neighbors' homes. With tears streaming down his cheeks, he tightened his grip on both of us. "Thank God your mother wasn't here to see this," he groaned, "and thank the Lord you're safe!"

Angry at the army for not protecting Lawrence, my father spent the first days brooding and vowing bureaucratic vengeance, determined to find out what security branch had failed and why. For long hours he would limp about the house, driving his fist into his palm and murmuring to himself about the "bitter end." He helped us slowly restore order around our place, cleaning up and repairing what he could. He allowed Mrs. Kreiger to move in with us, and she took up her usual chores without drunken George to scold. George's absence was conspicuous, and there was a sorrow in his wife that never seemed to fade away, though hard work served to occupy her by and by.

Of course, we told Pa about the priest hole and showed him where we'd hidden. We told him about the bargain Leah had made to save us. He listened intently but said very little, as if the weight of things was more than he could bear to talk about.

★

Within the month a government agent showed up at our house to assess our losses.

"We're making a full report of the degradation to the War Department in Washington," said the clerk. "Besides the looting of your home, is there anything specific you wish to claim? I understand a buckskin pony was stolen."

For the first time since his return, Pa burst forth with pent up anger. "A young *woman* was stolen!" he cried. "Do you think I care about a horse?"

The clerk departed quickly, pleading ignorance and backing out the door. "We weren't aware of any hostages. You can be certain that every Union regiment around is looking for Quantrill."

They wouldn't find him. Not that year or the next.

After the raid, Quantrill and his men faded back into Missouri, and while retribution was swift—raining down on Southerners along the border—the real perpetrators escaped. Union General Thomas Ewing ordered the inhabitants of three Missouri counties to be evacuated, giving the families fifteen days to leave and take all of their possessions with them. Jayhawkers, bent on revenge, dashed across the border to harass the refugees, robbing them and burning abandoned houses. But Quantrill himself remained at large, apparently idling away the remainder of the summer hiding out with his teenaged lover, Kate King, in Blue Springs, Missouri.

Where Quantrill's "soldiers" may have gone, no one really knew, but he gathered up four hundred of them in late September and headed for Texas, dealing more death and destruction along the way. They attacked a small Union fort at Baxter Springs, Kansas, in October and were still engaged when a ten-wagon supply train coming from the north proved a more inviting target. The wagons were escorted by a hundred soldiers and Major General James G. Blunt, Union commander of the Frontier District. The Bushwhackers sent a few men forward but kept most of their force hidden while they lured the federals into a trap, closing in and killing eighty-five men before looting and burning the wagons. General Blunt escaped to tell how even those who surrendered were gunned down in cold blood.

Quantrill's men reached Texas and then began fighting amongst themselves. George Todd and "Bloody Bill" Anderson split from the main group to lead factions of their own and compete with Quantrill for glory and notoriety. Anderson's outfit was especially brutal. Throughout the summer of 1864, he and his thugs killed and scalped their victims, usually young soldiers on patrol who fell into their hands.

In September Anderson and his men commandeered a train as it chugged into a station at Centralia, Missouri. They ordered the 125 passengers from the cars, including twenty-five Union soldiers going home on leave. These boys were unarmed but in uniform and soon found themselves encircled by a mob of drunk and cursing raiders who made them strip before they shot them, killing twenty-two of the helpless men.

Hearing news of these atrocities, I always pictured Lonnie Hodge and Rand Saugus present and wondered about Leah. Where was she? Was she cold and frightened? Had Saugus harmed her? Was she still alive? Sometimes I'd dream of seeing her and Taffy coming up the road, Leah leisurely walking the horse the way she sometimes liked to do at twilight. Once I could have sworn I actually saw her coming. I was on the porch listening to the birds and crickets as the sun went down. Suddenly, there was Leah leading Taffy up the road toward our gate. She wore a big straw hat, which had dropped to her shoulder, and a smile on her face that I could see a long way off. Her dark hair was long and pretty, still anchored by that single braid, loose on one side.

I almost jumped out of my chair. My mouth dropped open to call out, the first gasp catching in my throat. Then the girl and horse came sharper into focus, and I realized it wasn't Leah after all, only Mrs. Parry's spinster daughter coming home from evening choir practice.

Leah haunted me like that. I thought about her all the time. I half expected a postal card or letter from Joby Crockett, inquiring about Leah because of the raid and all. Nothing ever came. I tried not to hold that against Crockett—maybe he'd been killed or captured—but it gnawed at me that once Leah had rejected him, he really didn't care. Heaven help me, I still cared, more than I could ever say.

I began to see those summer days before the attack as the best part of my life. Sitting evenings on the porch, I remembered our last peaceful time together just before that terrible morning—me and Bobbie and Toe-Jam with Leah and Addie in the swing and a brilliant August sun hanging on the horizon just for us. I yearned to bring that moment back, and in my imagination that's exactly what I did. I could hear our laughter; I could see Leah's face, shining as she took in Bobbie's gentle teasing over Joby Crockett. Maybe it helped her get over Crockett that night, lightening things up the way Bobbie did. I was always glad I had that vision to remember, for Bobbie was in the graveyard and Leah never did come home.

★

I sorted through Leah's possessions while we were cleaning up her room for Mrs. Kreiger to move in. Among the tipped-over drawers and scattered papers, I found Leah's Book of Mormon. Soon after that, I set out to read it since it had meant so much to her. There was a lot I didn't understand, but its story involved a lost people heading toward the promised land.

I remembered the man Nephi from the story Leah had told about him being bound up during the storm. Once he was free, the compass worked again and the folks could get where they were going. I wondered if Leah would ever be free again, and if the holy compass would ever work for her. One verse in Nephi said, "And blessed are they who shall seek to bring forth my Zion at that day, for they shall have the gift and power of the Holy Ghost; and if they endure unto the end they shall be lifted up at the last day, and shall be saved in the everlasting kingdom of the Lamb."

Leah certainly sought to bring forth Zion. She had the gift and power of her faith. Would she be saved after death as the verse implied? I wasn't satisfied. I wanted Leah now, not after death. I didn't care about Zion. I wanted Leah to come home.

My father never returned to his regiment. His knee was shattered, which allowed him a medical discharge, but the destruction of

Lawrence was what really kept him home. The people needed him. So many able-bodied men were dead; so many widows were in mourning. Every hand was pressed into the work of making our town whole again. Pa directed the demolition of scores of burned-out businesses and homes. Despite his terrible limp, he helped our neighbors rebuild where they could, offering his own resources to buy pitch and paint and bricks and lumber. It was a slow process, but eventually Lawrence began to show signs of recovery, and by the time the war ended a year and eight months after the attack, we were a recognizable village once again.

The emotional scars would take longer to heal.

Addie began speaking more as time went on. Often I would find her studying the note cards Leah had made for her, sounding out the letters of the written words. Perhaps it was her way of hanging on to Leah, by practicing the drills and forcing herself to do what they'd both hoped for. "When Leah comes home, I want to show her how well I'm speaking," she'd tell me, and I would tousle her curls and smile at her improved vocabulary and enunciation.

The war ended in April of 1865. Robert E. Lee signed the articles of surrender at Appomattox in Virginia. General Grant accepted them, and the long nightmare was over. A few guerrilla bands like those of Anderson and Quantrill vowed to continue the senseless bloodshed, wreaking havoc on Union villages and outposts in spite of the South's surrender. But leaders on both sides pleaded for a "just and lasting peace," and cooler heads eventually prevailed. The most vicious of the Southern raiders were already in their graves. George Todd was killed fighting Jayhawkers a month after the Centralia massacre, shot through the neck by a sniper. Five days later, outnumbered and outgunned, Bloody Bill Anderson charged a troop of Union militiamen in northwestern Missouri and was shot off his horse with his guns still smoking.

William Clarke Quantrill was leading a group in Kentucky when the peace treaty was signed. Federal soldiers shot him a month later, probably remembering Lawrence, Kansas, as they took careful aim.

With the official end of the war, I thought that somehow Leah would come back, but she never did. Nor did we ever see Lonnie Hodge or Rand Saugus around Lawrence again. I figured they'd been killed or maybe imprisoned in Missouri. I sometimes leafed through wanted posters at the courthouse, hoping to find some clue about where they were or if they had survived. A lot of Bushwhackers turned to crime once the war was over, Frank and Jesse James among them. Most eventually wound up at the end of a hangman's noose or as the target of a lawman's bullet.

Toe-Jam and I were almost sixteen by then and sobered by both our memories of the massacre and our own maturing. I came to calling Toe-Jam just plain Toe more often or sometimes even Henry, in memory of Leah. He said that someday he hoped most folks would call him Mr. Kettle but that I could always call him Toe.

I planned to matriculate at the new University of Kansas, which had been established right in Lawrence. Following in my father's footsteps was what I had in mind. After witnessing such terrible violence, justice under the law seemed an honorable thing to study. Leah had taught me a love of books and language, so I looked on academics with some interest. Toe was good at working with his hands and leaned toward perfecting his mechanical skills, putting things together like gears and wheels. I admired his natural deftness. We remained good friends, but Bobbie was conspicuously absent, and traipsing around Lawrence in the summer was never quite the same as it once had been.

Mostly, I missed Leah. The sound of her screams that last day in the parlor flooded my dreams at night. The thought of what she'd done, what she'd sacrificed for me, gnawed at my heart. If I had idealized her before, I idolized her now. She lived in my imagination, beautiful as ever, and somehow working her way home.

Chapter Three

ALMOST FIVE YEARS HAD PASSED since the massacre when my father married Juliette Freeman's widowed sister, Rebecca Stoughton. Mrs. Stoughton's husband, Phillip, had been killed while running for safety through a cornfield that dreadful August day, leaving four children fatherless and Rebecca wearing black for the next two years. She was a strikingly attractive woman, robust and well proportioned, with fine features and a mass of lovely hair. My father began squiring her about not long after she entered Lawrence society again, and soon we were making room for Becca and her children in our home.

Addie, who had turned nine, was happy to have three new sisters, one near her age, and a younger brother to tease and tattle on. I was happy for my father and not surprised when he made a place in my mother's empty bedroom for the new Mrs. Pace. It was time for our home to come alive again. I liked Becca and was sincerely pleased that she was happy after all that she'd suffered. Still, when her oldest girl was given Leah's room and moved in with all the clamor of a teenaged goose—complete with flapping wings and feathers—it seemed a sacrilege. The sudden descent of all the Stoughtons made me uncomfortable, and I became restless and ready more than ever to answer some yearning that had haunted me for years. I was nineteen now, tall and strong, no longer a boy. I was old enough to choose my way.

At the wedding, a cousin of Becca's mentioned offhandedly that he had recently seen Lonnie Hodge in a little Missouri town he'd chanced to travel through. "I could never forget that face. Hodge looked older and as worn down and grimy as an old mongrel dog, but I knew it was him. Workin' in a blacksmith shop, he was. Covered in soot when I saw him, which is appropriate, I think, for the devil he is. He turned his eyes and cowered when he noticed me. I reckon all those old Bushwhackers do their best to avoid anybody from Lawrence. Someone ought to go and string those fellows up for what they done, though proving anything at trial would be a hard thing after all this time."

"We've moved on," replied my father. "Those boys are rotting in their own filth now."

The man nodded, and the conversation turned to other things, but I was stunned. "Where did you say you saw Lonnie Hodge?" I managed to ask before the man melted away into the crowd.

"Higginsville," he answered. "Higginsville, Missouri."

★

"Forget it, boy. It's a fool's journey to seek these fellows out." Annoyed and angry, my father paced the floor, stiff legged, slamming his fist into his palm. "The war is over, Ethan. Lawrence is recovering. We best put these things behind us."

"I can't. Not yet."

"Bobbie Martin's in the graveyard, Ethan. All your vengeance toward Hodge won't bring him back."

"It's not only Bobbie . . ."

"It's Leah, isn't it?" My father softened his tone and paused. He'd grown distinguished-looking since the war, with graying hair and the somber eyes of a battle veteran. The past still burdened him, and suddenly he broke and began speaking solemnly about it. "You blame me, don't you, for not going after Rand Saugus when I first came home, for not somehow finding that girl?" He looked me square in the eye. "You think I should have gone after them. You think I should have searched for Leah."

"She saved my life. I'd have been in the graveyard now with Bobbie if it weren't for her."

My father eyed me curiously. "Your mother's in that graveyard too. I wonder if, for a while, Leah didn't take your ma's place in your mind. That's why you bonded with her like you did."

"I don't know," I stuttered. "But it's gnawed at me for five years that no one's ever looked for Leah. I'm man enough to do it now, and I can't rest until I figure out what happened to her."

"You might not like what you find," my father murmured sadly.

"I've got to try, Pa. No matter what comes at the end of it."

My father thought a long time, pensively rubbing his chin. Then he put both hands on my shoulders. "You have my blessing, Ethan, and money too," he finally said. "I had a bad knee five years ago and a town to bring back from the ashes. Today I got a new wife and family to look after. But Leah Donaldson was an orphan in our charge. We owe her something. We needed to look out for her. I'm proud you're man enough to do it."

Addie came to me that night, tapping on my door on her way to bed. She'd become a flighty nine-year-old, with ringlets down her back and a faint spray of freckles across her nose. Since finding her voice, she had spent the last few years making up for lost time, always eager to talk, almost constantly. She was also fully immersing herself in the delight of having three new sisters whose noisy silliness only encouraged her to join the chatter. But now, Addie was quiet and demure as she settled herself in the rocking chair.

"Pa says you're going off to find Leah." She gave me that wide-eyed look she'd once had as a little girl. It reminded me of another time.

I nodded. "I'm going to try." I concentrated on the boot I was polishing, expecting some sort of objection since everyone else had initially responded to the plan by saying I was foolish.

"I wish I could go with you, Ethan."

I looked up from the boot and saw tears welling in Addie's eyes. Suddenly it all came back like a terrible black cloud. I looked at Addie and remembered her body shaking and her little fists gripping me in terror as we lay together in the priest hole five years before. Dropping the boot, I got up and moved toward her, drawing her to me. She leaned her face into my chest while I ran my fingers through her hair. "You remember, don't you?" I murmured.

"Tell Leah that I'm happy," she sobbed. "Tell her that I'm happy, and it's all because of her!"

"I'll do that, Addie. I promise you I will."

★ ★ ★ ★ ★ ★ ★ ★ ★ ★ ★ ★ ★ ★

A DAY LATER I FOUND Toe at the harness shop, where he had taken a job adjusting buggy springs for Jacob Ball. He was under a carriage on his back with oil dripping in his eyes when I came upon him.

"I'm going to Missouri," I said straight off. "I'm gonna get that Lonnie Hodge for what he did. I have an idea where he is, and I won't rest until I find him. It's been five years, Henry, but I can't let it go."

Toe slid out from under the buggy and stood looking at me with those same round eyes that used to endear him to Leah. Like me, he had grown up since the massacre and was now strong and able in his work. A little somber like the rest of us, he still had a spark of humor and a certain joy in living that I hadn't quite regained. "So you found ol' Lonnie's scent along some dusty road, and ya can't take leave of it."

"I got a bone to pick with Hodge," I answered grimly. "And so do you."

"You got that right." Toe hesitated, wiping his hands on his greasy apron. "You goin' after Lonnie Hodge, or are you hopin' to find Leah? She's the one you can't let go, now ain't she?"

"We got lots of reasons to find Hodge," I spit back, annoyed. "I'm inviting you to come along. Maybe Hodge can tell us where Leah is or what happened to her."

Toe slowly wiped his hands again and studied me. "Some things are best left alone," he said. "Some things you're better off not knowin'."

"This isn't one of them."

"You're bound and determined to head out?"

"I can't help it. I've got to find her."

He sized me up again and finally shrugged. "Well, I guess I'm goin' with ya then. Jake Ball's carriage springs'll have to wait." He removed his apron.

The next day the two of us were riding east toward Missouri.

The countryside had reawakened since the war. Much of it was green again, flourishing with an abundance of corn and wheat and pasture grass. Hay fields were pale in the summer sun. Stands of timber lined the streams of northwest Missouri, and only an occasional burnt-out shack or twisted bridge reminded us that the land had once been torn apart by cannon balls and grapeshot. Toe and I were mostly quiet as we rode along, lost in our own thoughts.

Henry had grown into a tall, smooth-featured man, handsome in his youth. Even in a checked shirt and a worn officer's hat, he looked strong in the saddle. We both had long-barreled revolvers, and Henry had a rifle. "It's a gift to us poor humans," he said, "how nature comes back rich and strong even when the world's turned upside down. Birds sing again. The creeks run by just like they used to. It's as though God always has another chance to give us, isn't it, Ethan?"

"Bobbie never had a second chance," I answered grimly.

"Leah might be waiting," he reminded me, "just like them meadow flowers had to wait for a change of seasons to blossom up again."

★

They didn't know Lonnie Hodge in Higginsville, Missouri, and they looked askance at Henry, who seemed well outfitted for a black man.

"Folks is wary of coloreds now they's free," an old teamster at a watering hole told us, eyeing Henry up and down. "They's high and mighty now, and some are thirstin' for revenge. Is that why yer lookin' for this Lonnie Hodge?"

"You don't have to be colored to crave a little justice," I told him.

"Don't know no fellow by that name," said the blacksmith when we found him, a brawny brute of a man who looked his part. He scowled and gestured menacingly with his fire poker. His bald head was wrapped in a red bandana. Beads of sweat ran down his face, and he made a point of showing off his muscle by lifting an iron bar out of the coals with one arm. "What you boys want with this Lonnie Hodge?"

"We knew him back in Kansas before the war," I said. "Someone told us he was here."

"He was a colored-lover, was he?" said the smith contemptuously, and Toe had to hold me back as my fists began to tighten.

We moved away before my temper got the best of me, and we circled around the back of the old smithy to look over the alleys of the town. It was easy to see that Higginsburg had no welcome mat for strangers, especially a black man and a Yankee. Many a slacker scowled in our direction as we found water for our horses and biscuits for ourselves. And when twilight settled in, the place grew eerie as the street lanterns winked and yellow windows lit the town.

The smoke was still rising through the chimney of the smithy when Toe and I saw three men walk under the eaves and disappear inside. We could hear the clang of iron and the crude roar of laughter as the newcomers bantered with the bald blacksmith before he closed up shop. We watched the brawny man finally leave with his three friends, heading straight for a diner down the block. The odd thing was, the shop was still lit up like a Christmas tree, and we could hear hammering inside. I motioned for Toe to follow me, and we went in to take a closer look.

There, all alone, was Lonnie Hodge, balding now and uglier than I remembered, pounding away on a horseshoe. I could hardly believe he was the same man I knew in Lawrence. The sight of him numbed me for a moment. So often had I wondered what a face-to-face with Lonnie would be like, and now here he was, the devil I had hated for so long.

He looked up at us, startled by our coming through the door—probably as stunned as we were. Then his dark eyes narrowed, and I saw a flame of recognition cross his face. Separately, Toe and I might not have been easily recognized, but together, folks remembered us as kids.

"Hey, Lonnie," I said, trembling with hate and fear and trying not to show it, "you remember me?"

"Name ain't Lonnie," growled Hodge warily. "I don't know no one by that name. If you ain't got business here, you better get on out."

In a flash I was on him, grabbing him by the collar. "Oh, I got business here, Lonnie Hodge. You can bet on that!"

Toe wrenched the hammer from Hodge's hand and helped me pull him into a corner away from the fire. The man was frantic and began to yell until I grabbed an oily rag and stuffed it in his mouth. He rocked and squirmed as I held him down, surprised at how small and shriveled he seemed to be. Toe caught the handle of the fire poker and drew it, burning hot, near Hodge's cheek. Lonnie went rigid, too stiff to move, as he followed the poker from the corner of his eye. I took the rag out of his mouth so he could talk. "Your name is Lonnie Hodge. Don't you deny it! You came riding into Lawrence in August 1863 and slaughtered innocent people in cold blood! You betrayed your town, killing folks who used to pass you on the street! You don't deserve to live!"

"We was under orders on that raid!" gasped Lonnie. "We was following Quantrill. Lawrence was a Union stronghold. We was told to burn it down!" His eyes bulged in terror, shining in the firelight.

"You killed Bobbie Martin!" I screamed. "He was my friend, and he was just a boy!"

"No, I never killed no boy. Others did, but I never shot no one."

"You were gonna put a bullet in *my* ear. I heard you say it!"

"It was all talk, just talk," he moaned.

"I suppose you never burned any houses either or used the back of your hand on Leah Donaldson." I tightened my grip on Hodge's throat, ready to choke him. Leah's screams that day in the parlor flooded back to me, and for a split second I was in the priest hole again, clinging on to Addie, my heart pounding against my chest.

"Leah Donaldson?" Hodge's eyes lit up.

"Where is she, Lonnie? Where did Saugus take her? You got one chance to save your sorry life."

Toe laid the poker closer to Hodge's jaw, and the man cried out and struggled to turn away. Toe pushed the poker closer. "One chance, Hodge. I swear I'll brand you like a Texas steer and quarter you for packin'."

"I ain't seen Saugus in five years," cried Hodge. "He's most likely dead by now, and that girl too, if you want to know. You Yankees made short work of Quantrill's boys once the war was over."

"Where was Saugus when you saw him last?" I shook Lonnie hard. "You tell me what you know while there's any breath left in ya."

Lonnie began to cry and then to sob. He was like a skinny old scarecrow in my hands. I almost felt sorry for him, seeing where his deeds had brought him.

Just then I heard the shatter and crash of wood beside me, and Toe sunk to the floor under the kindling of a broken chair. A huge arm circled round my neck, just below my chin, pulling me away from Hodge and tightening so I couldn't breathe. My hands flew to the fellow's wrist, scratching and tugging against his grip.

"What ya want me to do with 'im, Lon," the man's voice cackled in my ear, "rip his head off and throw 'im out the door? Or I can throw him head first in the fire if that's what ya want." His burly arm still around my neck, the man swung me like a limp toy toward the glowing forge.

The monster pushed my face toward the coals and held me there while I jerked and fought and closed my eyes. The heat was searing. The pain was more than I could bear. I screamed and struggled before the man suddenly pulled me from the heat.

"No, Tyke, let 'im be. Don't burn 'im." Lonnie was pleading for my life.

I fell to my knees, gasping for breath as the man dropped me on the ground. I could smell my singed hair. My cheeks and forehead were so hot I was afraid to touch them. Painfully, I slid backward into the farthest corner from the forge and tried to find cool air. Toe was lifting himself off the floor, staggering under the blow he'd suffered. I watched him hopefully until the big blacksmith crossed between us, towering over me.

"You got nerve comin' around here, boy," he said. "Weren't for Lonnie, I'd a-fried ya." He stepped aside, laughing softly in a mocking way. "Whatever you got against ol' Lon, you oughta thank 'im now. Another second and I'd a burned that handsome young face a yours so ya couldn't show up no more in public. You come snoopin' round a blacksmithy, that's what yer gonna git!"

"Leave 'im be, Tyke," repeated Hodge, who was still gathering his own wits after being choked.

"What's these boys want with you, Lonnie?" asked Tyke. "Somethin' leftover from the war?" Hodge didn't answer, and finally the blacksmith shrugged and moved toward the front of the stone shack where it opened under the eaves. "I'll leave ya to yer troubles, then," he said. "Seems like the fight's drained outta 'em. I can do that to most men, 'specially near a fire."

When he was gone, Lonnie looked from Toe to me and back again, still nervous. "Tyke's my boss," he finally offered quietly. "He come to my defense is all. He never meant no harm."

I was in too much pain to answer him, and for a while I just sat there, wishing for the sting on my skin to go away. It was hot and smoky in the room, and I could hardly breathe. The big blacksmith was right. The fight had drained right out of me.

Suddenly Hodge began to sob again. He held his head in his hands and wiped his eyes, and his body trembled. "I'll be haunted by what I done in Lawrence till the day I die. I see the burnin' in my dreams. I hear the shrieking of the people in my sleep. I can't never let it go."

"It oughta haunt you," I spat at him. "It oughta haunt your every waking thought! Hell is waiting for you, Hodge, for what you did in Lawrence."

"Hell ain't waitin'," he answered miserably. "I'm there already."

"Why'd you make that blacksmith pull Ethan from the fire?" Toe spoke up.

"'Cause I'm sorry for what I done and I couldn't bear no more pain for anyone from Lawrence. You may not believe me, but it's true. I didn't kill your friend, but I was part of awful deeds that haunt me to this day."

"Tell me what happened to Leah Donaldson," I demanded. "If you're so sorry, help me find her."

"I don't know that I can. It was Saugus who took that girl. The boys flew out in all directions after the raid on Lawrence. I ain't sure where Saugus ended up."

"You're still lyin' to me! You were Saugus's hired man. You knew his business. He'd make a point to keep in touch." I was in his face again.

Hodge cowered in front of me. "I swear I don't know what become of Saugus and the gal. Once I heard Saugus showed up in Cole County after the war, but that's all I know!"

"Cole County?"

"It's east a ways around Jefferson City. The Missouri River runs right through it."

I couldn't believe him about Saugus. I leaned back and stared at him. The terrible knowledge that this poor, bedraggled man knew nothing about Leah began to settle over me, and I felt like sobbing too. I was tired and in pain, and so was Toe. We hung our heads and closed our eyes in resignation, barely noticing when Hodge moved through the shadows and slipped out the door. No one knew where Leah was.

Outside we found a back corner near the smithy to hunch over and get our wits about us. We stayed there, not knowing what to do.

I had drifted off to sleep when Lonnie came again, kneeling down beside me in a kindly way. I jerked awake and immediately reached up to defend myself, but he let me know there was no need.

"I got something for you, Ethan," Lonnie said quietly, and Toe moved across to us, curious about the candle the man held. "Maybe this will prove that I told you all I know about that girl. And I hope you find her."

There in his hand he held my mother's pendant dangling on a chain. The flame of the candle accented the ivory oval's loveliness. I swallowed hard, too mesmerized to speak.

"One of the fellows took this when we ransacked yer house," said Lonnie. "I bought it from 'im for half a dollar 'cause I knew where it was he got it. I figured I could make a profit tradin' it to Saugus, but I never got the chance. Then I didn't want to part with it once I thought of what I'd done. It was like I'd saved something beautiful from that awful day—in spite of all I'd taken."

I took the proffered pendant, sliding it from his dirty fingers. If I had come to kill this man, the pendant had just saved his life.

"I wouldn't be giving you that necklace if I didn't care," Hodge whispered hoarsely. "When you first come, I fought and lied 'cause I was scared. The truth is, I've been waitin' for someone from Lawrence to show up. I'm ready for anything ya want to do to me. It's the only way I might find any peace."

We left him there, his head bowed, his shoulders drooping. I didn't have forgiveness in me, but neither did I need to punish Lonnie with my fists or my rope or my revolver. He would suffer until he died without my touching him.

With only Hodge's vague notion about Cole County, Toe and I cleaned up and headed there, weary and without much hope but still determined. The thought of Leah ending up in the same wretched conditions as Lonnie haunted us as we pushed on. Finding Lonnie didn't bring Bobbie back or even avenge his death, but I still had hope for Leah. Along a dozen country roads, behind a score of fences, barns, and outposts, in thick stands of trees and under bridges, I prayed every night that we would find her and that somewhere she was still alive.

Chapter Five

⭐ ⭐ ⭐ ⭐ ⭐ ⭐ ⭐ ⭐ ⭐ ⭐ ⭐ ⭐ ⭐ ⭐

WE ARRIVED IN COLE COUNTY the last week in May and searched the court records and census lists in Jefferson City for several days. There was nothing to give us any clue about Rand or Leah. We took to stopping at churches and post offices in small towns, inquiring at wayside gatherings and even at farmhouses we chanced to see. No one had heard of Leah, and few would admit to any knowledge of the whereabouts of former Bushwhackers and raiders. Many Missourians were related to those who fought guerrilla style, and they kept those secrets.

With the curiosity and wanderlust of boys, Toe and I turned east, making our way to St. Louis, the largest city in Missouri and the bustling crossroads point in the flourishing Midwest. For the first time in my life, I saw a busy, throbbing city with tree-lined, cobbled streets in all directions and a skyline filled with chimneys. The center of the town was rife with commerce as Mississippi River traffic converged from north and south and railroad lines from all points east terminated there. Filled with wonder, we walked the streets and took in the marvels of all we saw—from shops and stores where saddles, hats, and fine boots beckoned, to the restaurants and clubs that offered music and sometimes a play act with our meals.

To this point we had camped on the road, usually finding some isolated river cove or forest glen, just a place to build a fire and wrap in our bedrolls for the night. In St. Louis we decided to treat ourselves to a nice hotel, with clean sheets and a bathtub for a change. No coloreds were allowed in the best places, but I told the clerk that Toe was my manservant, and he let us register. We were given a room with a small valet's quarters included and came out better than we bargained for. Toe and I laughed about it later. I gave him the main bed and apartment, preferring the other space because it had an extra lamp. I was happy to give up the bigger bed.

"Ethan," Toe said, sprawling on the wide, four-post bed and into the billowy pillows, "this big a bed isn't new to me, ya know. We had one like it at home. The difference was, there was five of us kids in it at one time! I might get lost here in all these covers with no one to bump into! You sure you don't want me to take that little cot in the servant's quarters, just so I'll know where I am in the morning?"

I threw a pillow at him and left him laughing on the king-sized bed.

We recovered for a couple days in that hotel, nursing the aches and pains of travel, and on the second morning, reading the St. Louis newspaper by the side of my toast and eggs, I saw a notice that caught my interest.

Joseph Spenser
Ox Team Agent
Utah Territory

Beneath the headline was an address near the docks, and we determined to find the place that very day. It was the first I'd seen or heard of Utah in five years. I knew it had nothing to offer *us*, that simple word, but its connection to Leah's Zion made me suddenly determined to search out the ox team agent. It was all we had, the word *Utah* jumping out at me in black newsprint. Did this man organize wagon companies bound for the Rocky Mountains? Was he a Mormon? If so, what was he doing in Missouri where the Mormons were still hated? The single word and all these questions. It was all we had.

★

We searched about the docks, through the spate of rabbit hutches that passed for the "apartments" that provided crowded space for commerce along the riverfront. Most inquiries got us nothing but a shrug until one old sailor lit up when I mentioned Joseph Spenser's name.

"Oh, he's the Lord's own agent!" said the man. He pointed out directions with a gnarled, shaking finger. "An agent of the Lord, that's what Spenser is," he repeated, sending us on our way.

We found Joseph Spenser in the dusty closet of an office hidden behind other, more respectful-looking spaces. He was a younger man than I expected, in his early thirties with light curly hair, piercing blue eyes, and a heavy blond mustache. His ready smile was disarming, as was his appearance. He dressed like a teamster rather than a business-man and wore a fringed leather coat of the Western plains and heavy boots that reached almost to his knees. He looked to be lean and strong and in his prime, a fellow you'd like on your side in a fight. He greeted us with a quick handshake and the offer of two chairs.

"I could use two strapping fellows," he told us generously, "though my trail jobs usually go to Mormon boys who are already with the company. They can help their families that way. You fellows wouldn't be part of this last group of emigrants, would you?"

"We're not looking for a job," I told him. "We saw you were Utah bound and wondered about it. We had a friend once, a woman who we lost track of during the war. She was set on going to Utah someday, said it was her Zion." I shrugged, feeling a bit foolish. "She may be in Missouri. We saw your notice and hoped you might know any Mormons here."

"The war was a long time ago, and most of the Mormons left even before that. What makes you boys think your friend is here?"

"She was taken by folks headed to Missouri. That's all we know. It's a long shot, coming here."

"Must be important to you," said Spenser, measuring us in a friendly way. I didn't answer right off, and he swung around in his chair to the roll-top desk that took up most of the room. From a pile of papers he drew a dog-eared map and turned to face us once again. "I'm an agent for what the Church calls its Perpetual Emigration Fund. We've got literally thousands of converts coming every year, mostly from England and Scandinavia plus folks from the Eastern states—Pennsylvania, New York, Massachusetts, all of 'em. Like your friend, they're all wanting to get to Zion. With its fund, the Church pays these people's way, and then they work off the bill once they're in the valley."

Spenser stood for a moment to peer out of the small, smudged window near his desk. Then he turned back, obviously happy to talk about his job. "The railroad ends here in St. Louis, so folks come this far by train." He pointed to St. Louis on the map. "From here they need an ox team and a wagon and a company to travel with. That's what I'm for. I meet the trains and arrange for these homeless folks to cross the prairie, hopefully before the weather changes."

"What happens if they can't?"

"Well, it takes some doin' to get 'em started. I'll admit to that. Sometimes we have to find lodging for 'em here for a few weeks. A lot depends on the season. If I can get 'em outta here by mid-June, they got a chance at not bein' stuck here or up the road somewhere. Trouble is, we don't go through Missouri. We have to put these people on a riverboat and send 'em up to Iowa to begin the crossing. We have outposts across Iowa and some more help around Council Bluffs and Florence."

I listened eagerly, remembering Leah's speaking of these places, saying that she had once lived there.

"There's wagonmakers and cartwrights along that trail and ox traders too. We've contracted with 'em and know their skills." He turned to the map again and traced his finger along the bottom of Iowa, showing us the route. "We cut right along here, and then Nebraska lies in wait and we head for the Platte River, hopin' to make good time. The prairie's green and lush along the river, grass we wish for later on."

"Do you go with these companies?"

"Not usually," said Spenser. "I stay here to coordinate things. But this June I'm goin'. I haven't been home in over a year, so I'm takin' the season's last company to the valley. I'm hopin' to find a wife if you want to know the truth. If I don't have good luck there, I'll come back here again next spring and help the emigrants again."

"How many will there be?" I asked, admiring this man's enthusiasm for such an arduous journey.

"Oh, I imagine we'll have some ten wagons in our group, maybe fifty or sixty people, counting kids and babies. I'm meetin' a train here in two days, and I hope to get them all to Keokuk by next week sometime. These last are stragglers. We'll join the main party on the road in Iowa."

"How many times you done this?" asked Toe, interested.

"Oh, lots of times. Mormon converts have kept the road to Zion well worn ever since the forties. Great, great souls, they are! Some of 'em give up everything, ya know. A lot of 'em are disowned by their friends and families. They have to cross an ocean and spend weeks more on a train. There's no rest once they make it to St. Louis either. Mountains and deserts lie ahead, some 1,300 miles. Most will have to walk a great deal of the way. It's their faith that pushes them, ya know. They believe in the promises of Zion, and it's quite a thing to see."

Spenser paused, letting his words hang in the air for a moment. "They say there'll be a rail line clear across the country in a year or two," he finally remarked. "That's bound to make things easier. For now, all these folks have is that faith I spoke of, faith in God and faith in me. I'm on God's errand. I've got to do my part."

The image of Nephi on the ship came back to me, the story Leah had read to us so long ago. Faith provided the power on that journey, too, to another promised land.

"Leah—the girl we're looking for—was hoping to go to Zion," I told Spenser. "What is it that makes so many people risk everything for the middle of a wilderness?" I had asked Leah a similar question when I was just a boy, but I wanted to hear Spenser's take on things.

"You've got to know the fervor of the gospel to understand such need," he answered. "Ours is a religion of divine revelation. Once you've felt the power of the Holy Ghost and have truly been converted, there's no going back. Zion becomes the gathering place where your children can be born and raised with people of the covenant. Of course, it's also an idea as well as a specific place. In some ways Zion is anywhere a child of God finds peace."

The fellow was sounding a bit like Leah in his descriptions of this utopia beyond the mountains. For a brief moment, it crossed my mind to cynically tell him that for all her faith, Leah lost her Zion the day God forgot to cast His grace on Lawrence, Kansas. But I held my tongue. Joseph Spenser was warm and engaging, a pleasure to listen to—and he was obviously full of a robust faith. He reminded me of Leah in his encompassing and interested compassion. Perhaps all Mormons were that way.

"I'm sorry to say we've had no Leah Donaldson come through here. This is where folks come looking for help getting to the West. I keep a record of the names, and I think I'd remember her, from what you say." Spenser had walked to the door and accompanied us on a short stroll across the docks. He seemed to sense how crucial finding Leah was to two boys barely gone from home.

"I have a feeling," he said, "you should go back to Cole County. This time, tell everyone you meet that you're looking for a Mormon girl. I think your Leah would have left her mark in people's minds if they ever came across her, and it would be because of her religion, which brightens the faces of the best of us, even in troubled times."

"Missourians aren't known to care for Mormons very much," I reminded him. "Maybe we'd be better off not mentioning the name."

"It's a risk, and you can suit yourself," said Spenser. "But I'm bettin' this girl left a good impression, no matter where she went, and her faith was part of it."

We left him then, the "Lord's own agent." He waved his hand and wished us luck, and we returned the salutation. "That Spenser is a noble fella, ain't he?" said Toe as we walked away. "There's a generous, cheerful nature in 'im like Leah used to have. Maybe he knows best when he says we oughta talk about her being Mormon if these folks stand out like they do."

The next day we turned toward Cole County again, and I was determined to follow that advice.

Chapter Six

We were still scouring Cole County by late June, fearlessly announcing our purpose to anyone who would listen. "We're looking for a Mormon girl who was kidnapped from Kansas during the raid on Lawrence. Does anyone know of any Mormons hereabouts?" We got all kinds of responses, mostly bitter and uncouth. Some folks still worshipped William Clarke Quantrill and considered the Lawrence massacre a victory of war. Any of its victims deserved everything they got. Other people said that if Leah was a Mormon, she had no business in Missouri and she'd better keep her religion to herself or face the consequences.

"Our governor issued an extermination order against them Mormons over twenty-five years ago," shouted one old codger. "And it still stands today as far as I'm concerned. Them Mormons brought the devil here. In '39, I could shoot a Mormon on the spot and get a medal for it!"

"The surviving soldiers of the Lawrence raid are hid all over," a preacher in Annisburg told us. "They keep a low profile now, since the war was lost, but they're heroes here among the people who are proud to keep their secrets. As the years have passed, the raiders have melted into the population, and I suppose any of their women have done the same. The war did no good for Missouri. The poor folks are still poor. A man still has to sweat to make a livin'. And now free slaves compete for any work there is." He eyed Toe scornfully. "Mormons and coloreds—we don't like 'em in Missouri."

There were others who were kinder, especially some of the women—a farmer's wife here, a shop mistress there. Some even praised us for our efforts.

"Well, ain't that commendable," rasped one old widow who we encountered carrying baskets of vegetables down a country lane. "Two young fellows like you lookin' for a long-lost house servant. The war brought out the worst and best in people; that's all I've got to say." The woman invited us to her clapboard shack, where she fried up some grits and ham and let us wash in her well bucket. She served Toe a second helping and didn't seem to mind at all that he was black. It struck me how often it was that the people who had very little were often kinder and more giving than those who had more than what they needed.

On the road again, we found trouble dogging us in the next small town. Three young rowdies took exception to our asking about Mormons at the post office, and the local sheriff was sent for.

"You got nerve sniffing for your kind around here," said a snarly teenaged fellow, giving me a shove. "My grandpa run you devils out of Jackson and Clay Counties twenty years ago, and we don't want ya back!"

Toe stepped up to defend me, setting tempers to a boil.

"What you want, blacky?" cried one of the other boys, spitting hatred. I'd have punched him right there if a paunchy man with a mustache and a badge hadn't intervened.

"You go on home, Craythorn," the sheriff bellowed. "You too, Stitch. Go on, get outta here. You don't need trouble with these boys." He added weight to his words by having his deputy escort the mischief-makers down the street, and then he turned to Toe-Jam and me. "There ain't no Mormons here," he said, but there was goodwill in his eye. He introduced himself as Marcus Collier and looked us over with genial interest. "Is that what you boys are, missionaries or something? You've got a tough bunch of heathens here, if that's the case."

"We're not Mormons." I went on to explain about the search for Leah. He listened quietly and then apologized for the behavior of the boys. When he left us, I had the feeling it was with a good impression.

At dinner that night in a local café, we chanced to see Stitch and Craythorn and the other boy again. Still angry, they'd been shadowing us since the deputy let them go, and now they lurked around the door of the eatery, scowling at us, spitting in the street, and making vulgar comments to themselves. We kept an eye on these troublemakers as we ate, knowing they were itching for a tussle. They assumed I was a Mormon, and they were bound to punish me because of it. Well, I wasn't going to take it. Standing up to them would be the same as standing up for Leah. My fists were as hard as Toe's, and so was my disposition. Suddenly I realized what it felt like to be singled out and threatened because of religious prejudice, hated simply for being a Mormon or a Jew or one of those Catholics that used to hide in the priest holes of England. Just as Henry had lived under the scourge of racism, I felt the sting of this other senseless cruelty that had once left Leah's family on a frozen riverbank and forced thousands of others into the wilderness.

Henry and I ate our dinner with slow pleasure and then stood up with fire in our eyes. The boys had disappeared from the restaurant door, but we knew they weren't far away.

The street lay in shadows with few people about. Streaks of yellow gleaming from the diner's shuttered windows was all the light we had, but we moved defiantly, almost eager for what lay ahead. At the first corner past the door, it all began. The fellow called Stitch grabbed Toe from behind, wrapping a thick arm around his neck and pulling him backward. Before I could spring in to help, a tight fist struck my jaw, sending me to the ground with a savage animal soon on top of me. While the first fellow held me down, another kicked me in the ribs, landing mostly glancing blows as I squirmed and rolled to dodge him.

Grabbing his boot, I hung on like a bloodhound until he lost his balance and fell sprawling in the mud. The other boy was still trying to hammer me around the face and shoulders with his fists. A wild kid, he shrieked and sputtered as he fought. He used up his energy in anger, seldom landing any blows. He was scrappy but lighter and younger than I was, and soon I managed to throw him off. Toe-Jam had made short work of Stitch once they tumbled over. Using his elbows and feet, he struggled out of the fellow's grip and scrambled from under Stitch, knocking him back as he tried to rise.

We had the upper hand and would have easily sent these two whimpering away, but Craythorn, the man I'd tripped, came back at us with a knife he was bent on using. He took a swipe in my direction, his dark eyes flashing like the blade, and I backed up, turning cold. He advanced and was about to pounce again when an angel showed himself in the form of Sheriff Collier, who came striding between us, pistol drawn. I was never so glad to see a familiar face, even if it was a Missouri man.

"I told you, Craythorn. Leave these boys alone!" Collier bellowed, knocking the blade from the bully's hand and kicking it away. "An evening in my jail might serve to cool ya off if my warning doesn't do it!" The sheriff holstered his gun and used his bulk and authority to begin pushing Craythorn up the street. "Go on home. You too, Stitch! Get on outta here! Ben Petrie, you follow right behind. Go home and nurse that black eye. It'll puff up like a witch's bloom by morning. These fellows got the best of ya. It's time to give it up and part in peace."

The three rowdies limped off, scowling at Collier and muttering profanities over their shoulders. The sheriff only smiled and leaned down to retrieve the knife he'd kicked away. "I knowed them three since they was born. They're all bound for a hangman's noose if they don't mend their ways." He looked thoughtfully at the knife, turning it in his hands. "I figured they'd catch up with you fellows tonight, so I stayed on the prowl. Hope they didn't hurt ya none."

Toe was looking for his hat, and I was dusting off my clothes. "We held our own against the three of 'em till the knife came out," I told him. "We're grateful you stepped in."

The lawman looked us over once again and paused. His eyes were soft and bright like a father's might have been. "Actually, I was hopin' to find you boys still eatin' dinner. I've been thinkin' over your questions about that Mormon girl." The three of us were walking toward a sidewalk bench by then, and Collier motioned for us to sit as he kept talking. "I had to transport a body up to Clifton about a year ago. It's almost a ghost town, Clifton is, with no more than a rail stop and two or three hardscrabble shacks. But the deceased was to be buried there in the family plot. He was a thief and cutthroat, no good to anyone. Strong drink had mostly killed him before a bounty hunter's bullet found its mark. There was no one to mourn for him in Clifton, so me and my deputy Tom Skoal dug his grave ourselves once we found the proper spot."

Collier put his foot up on the bench and leaned against it. "I've buried men before in isolated places," he murmured, "but none so wretched as that."

"What you getting at? What's this got to do with Leah?"

"Well, nothin' maybe." He paused as if remembering some far-off scene. "That graveyard was completely empty of any living soul except for Tom and me. And then this young gal appears out of nowhere carrying some flowers. She was thin and pale and looked half starved, but there was a beauty to her. She had these flowers she had picked and asked if she could put 'em on the grave once we got it covered. I asked if she knew the man, and she confessed that she had no idea who he was.

"'Everyone deserves some words,' she said. 'I'd like to speak some for him if you'd let me.'

"Well, I told her that she could, and when we got the grave covered up, she stood there at the head and quoted what sounded like some scripture. Only it was no Bible verse that I had ever heard."

"Do you remember what she said?"

"Well, not word for word. But it was something about the spirit and the body being reunited again perfectly and this happening to everybody, the wicked and the righteous—Christ loosening the bands of death so that all of us can rise from the dead and stand before God and be judged. It was how she said those words that affected me. It was as if an angel spoke them. I asked her where that was in the Bible, and she said it wasn't a Bible verse she was reciting from memory but something from a book of her own people."

Collier stood on two feet again and shuffled around a bit to take in the June starlight. "I'm not a particularly religious man, but I never forgot the feeling I got when I heard those words, and it dawned on me today when you asked about a Mormon girl, if that wasn't what she was, that woman. Them Mormons have a book of scripture all their own, I think."

I wanted to weep on Sheriff Collier's shoulder. Instead, I looked into his fatherly eyes and thanked him from the bottom of my heart.

Clifton was fifty miles west, and the sheriff was there to see us off come morning after providing cots for sleeping and feed for our horses in a little stable he owned. It might as well have had a manger for the symbol of light and hope it was to me.

Chapter Seven

THE GOOD SHERIFF WAS RIGHT about Clifton. It was a beaten-down collection of shacks near a riverbed, where spring flooding left a swath of gravel every year. There were few trees to frame the hillsides or shade the open spaces, which looked like barren wasteland. Still, for all the ugliness we faced, for the grim little row of dugouts we were directed to beyond the cemetery, my heart began to pound against my chest at the thought of seeing Leah, and I could hardly breathe.

The houses were no more than a few boards and stones built against a gentle hill where caves had been dug to extend the space inside. Stove pots at several fire pits told us that the cooking was done outdoors. Tubs for bathing or washing clothes also stood nearby with buckets for hauling water stacked around them.

The entrances to most of the dugouts were covered with tarps or pieces of canvas. A few had rickety doors set in against a frame or hinged unevenly to a post. There were five of these shacks along the hillside, and probably more farther down, but when I asked an old woman lounging by her door about "the Mormon girl," she pointed wordlessly toward the end of the row, waving a heavy arm.

Toe and I found the last place in the row, a shanty pressed in against the hill, its entrance shaded by a pale-blue drape of cotton hung on a curtain rod. There was something pretty about the piece in spite of all the squalor so nearby. I lifted the cloth and peered inside to find a small, sparsely furnished room, windowless, quaint, and covered in shadows. "Hello? Is anybody here?" I swallowed hard and listened, but there was no response. Flies buzzed near the door, and a cow in a nearby pasture bellowed, but the room was silent and deserted.

Toe tapped me on the shoulder, and we both moved back into the sunshine, looking about the surrounding yard for any kind of life. At one corner of the house where the boards jutted out to form an edge, a garden patch came into view. It was a large, flat acre with several furrowed rows of vegetables and raspberry bushes along an ancient fence. Drawn at first by the relative abundance of the garden, I failed to see the figure with a hoe until Toe nudged my shoulder. "Look there," he said.

The woman's back was to us, and she wore a wide, ribboned, straw hat that covered her hair and hid the profile of her cheeks. We stood and watched her for a moment, and when she turned slightly toward us, my heart caught in my throat.

It was Leah. She hadn't looked our way, and I couldn't see her face, but I knew her. I could tell by the way she moved, by the way she leaned her shoulder against the hoe, by the way her hands slid up and down the handle as they found their grip. She was thin, almost gaunt, and wore a cotton dress of faded color. Her forearms were bare and burnished by the sun.

For a moment I was dumbstruck by the vision. I couldn't speak. I might have stayed there, stock-still in my tracks, if Toe hadn't pushed me forward. He was grinning wide, and his eyes were full of joy, like mine. Suddenly we were cutting through that garden on the run.

Hearing us, Leah turned, puzzled and curious before some light of recognition struck her. For one split second she seemed terror stricken and frozen where she stood. Then she dropped the hoe, and her hands flew to her mouth, and I heard a gasp of joy that's stayed with me all my life. She lurched toward us, losing her hat and its ribbons along the way.

"Ethan! Henry! Oh, it can't be you! It can't be you! Oh, Ethan! You're alive!"

Our arms were suddenly around her, holding her, loving her, pressing her close. We were all trembling and laughing and wiping away tears. Leah sobbed like a child. She clung to us, gripping our collars, running her fingers through Toe's hair, cupping my face in her hands. "Oh, Ethan, Henry," she repeated. "I can't believe you're here!"

"We're here, Miss Leah," laughed Toe, "all the way from Lawrence."

"Look at you!" she cried. "You're all grown up! When I left you, you were boys! Oh, how handsome you've both turned out to be!"

I could hardly speak. Leah looked weary. She looked older. She was pale, her cheekbones high and sharp, her hair bound up, not flowing freely anymore. I missed the single braid, which no longer framed her face, and her girlish dimples had all but disappeared. But her eyes, those dark, lustrous eyes, hadn't lost their shine. The warm embrace was still the same. She was my Leah once again.

"How did you ever find me?" she asked as we walked toward her house. "It's been five years. Surely Lawrence forgot me long ago. And the raid! Oh, that day!" She turned suddenly to me. "Addie? Is Addie all right? Oh, tell me about dear Addie!"

"Addie's fine," I laughed, "and talking too. You wouldn't believe it! She's become a real orator at all of nine years old!" I hesitated, unsure about setting a somber tone. "Addie said to tell you that she's happy, really happy, and it's all because of you and what you did for us. She loves you for it, Leah, and she always will."

Leah gripped my wrist. "It means the world to finally know . . ." Her voice trailed off, and I remembered that until this moment, our fate had been as much a mystery to Leah as hers had been to us.

She was still holding on to both our arms as we approached her "door." About to take us in, she paused. Her shoulders drooped and her smile faded. "It's awfully small inside. You tall boys will have to duck."

Sensing her embarrassment, Toe backed away, tipping his hat. "I'll just go get the horses. You and Ethan have lots to talk about."

The little room opened up as Leah lit a lamp. There was a small table with two chairs, a tin basin for washing, and a dingy mirror. The place was bare of most necessities, but a woman's touch was evident. The hard dirt floor was brightened by three woven scatter rugs, and Leah had put flowers on the table by a stack of dog-eared books. I caught the smell of violets in the air. The bedding was tucked neat and tight on a thin mattress in the corner, and the pillows were lumpy but clean. Another curtain hung on the back wall, covering some kind of doorway, perhaps a closet or another room. Leah began to smile again, fussing around to make a place for me. "As I said, there's hardly space enough for someone who's grown so tall." She laughed self-consciously. "But I'm *so* glad you're here it doesn't matter!"

Standing there, looking at the dingy room where Leah lived, I couldn't help myself. I took hold of this woman I loved, stopping her from nervously pushing chairs aside and straightening the rugs. I pressed her head against my shoulder, let her weep there in my arms, and told her she need never fret again. Things would be all right.

She looked up, and I saw in her eyes affection of the purest kind. "Oh, Ethan, thank God for you," she said. "Thank God you survived."

I was about to kiss her, full and in earnest, as Joby Crockett had once done, when suddenly I heard a sound coming from the curtained space on the dark side of the room. In utter shock, I instantly dropped my hands and stepped away from Leah. A small child, a girl with unruly brown hair, stood staring at us, wiping her sleepy eyes with one tight little fist. "Mama?" she said.

Leah didn't move but called the little girl to her. "Come, Gracie. Come meet Mama's friend."

The child remained wary. Leah looked at me and saw my shock turn to a scowl.

"Rand Saugus?" I whispered, stiffening.

Leah nodded, dropping her eyes, tears rolling down her cheeks.

"I'll kill him!" I gritted my teeth and spit the words so the child couldn't hear, but I felt my fists harden and my mouth go dry.

At that moment the little girl dashed into her mother's arms, and Leah tousled her curls. "There's my girl! She's not afraid of company! Did you take a nice long nap, my angel, and dream of pretty things?"

"Yes, Mama."

Leah knelt to the girl's level and pointed at me. "This is Mr. Ethan Pace from Kansas. Your mama knew him years ago, and his sister too. We all lived together in a fine house with fields and trees around it and a river not far away." She lifted the child and kissed her cheek. "Can you tell Mr. Pace your name?"

"Gracie," said the girl, quickly hiding her face in her mother's chest.

"Actually," Leah told me, "it's Adelyn Grace. I named her after Addie, but I call her Grace. She's been a treasure to me since I lost Addie."

Carefully, I stooped and took the youngster in my arms as Leah continued, happily praising her.

"She's four years old, and she can write her name already, can't you, Gracie? Mama showed you how to make the letters."

The girl was warm and small against me, and soon she was comfortable, laughing and giggling and pulling on my sparse chin whiskers. I saw Leah's features in her face, although her hair was not as dark nor her eyes as brown. I saw Saugus's shadow too and could hardly bear the image.

Toe and I had a good-sized piece of salted pork with us, and Leah cooked our dinner at the outdoor fire pit, adding vegetables to make a stew. The twilight air was mellow; a pale moon soon rose in the western sky. The coals of cooking fires glowed up and down the row of shacks. We heard voices but saw no neighbors.

Toe held Gracie on his lap and told her stories about him being a pig-tailed Topsy in Leah's *Uncle Tom's Cabin* production with Addie as Little Eva.

Gracie, still in awe of both of us, listened attentively but failed to see the joke. "Who's Topsy and Little Eva?"

I realized she was too young for the tale. She endeared herself to Toe though, asking sheepishly about the Confederate patch he wore, the one he'd "stolen" from my house the night we'd played Blind Burglar that summer long before. It reminded me we hadn't yet told Leah about Bobbie—and she was apparently afraid to ask.

We went back in the house after Gracie had been put to bed. Toe and I sat around the lamp with Leah. Its glow lit our faces and gave Leah's a fresh hue, like an old sepia-toned photograph, amber against a darkened room. I spoke quietly. "First, I need to tell you that Addie wanted to come with us. She followed me down the road, blowing kisses for you when I left."

Leah was delighted. "Oh, I'm so thrilled." She laughed.

"And even though she has new sisters, she still rules our house!"

Leah laughed heartily. "Of course she does!" Then her smile faded. "Thank heaven you both survived. I know so many didn't."

"Bobbie Martin was killed that day," I said gently, "shot down in his blue uniform on the path to Detmer's Grove." Leah covered her mouth, and her eyes widened. "I hate to tell you more," I whispered, my voice breaking a little.

"Tell me, Ethan. I need to know."

"Old George Krieger was killed before Greta could find him. So was your friend Judge Louis Carpenter—and Amos Willard, Mr. Fitch, Mr. Sullivan, Reverend Snyder. All of them."

"Louis Carpenter? Oh, Ethan!"

"It was a bitter thing for Mary, as you can rightly guess."

Toe piped up, "Mayor Collamore suffocated hiding in his well while his house burned, and the man who went down with him died too."

"Dear God," breathed Leah. "All of them?"

"One hundred fifty men in all," I told her. "Scores of homes and businesses burned. Lawrence was devastated. In five years it's barely coming back."

Leah was silent, trembling.

"My father came home after the massacre with a bad wound in the leg. He set about with others to rebuild. He married Rebecca Stoughton, who was left a widow by the raid. Her children fill our house now, and Addie has new sisters to keep her happy, as we told you. But a new family takes some getting used to, even if it's for the best."

"Thank God they didn't burn the house that day," said Leah. "I was so afraid they would. I should never have put you and Addie in the priest hole. I've agonized about it often. It was a terribly stupid thing to do."

"You saved our lives!" I grabbed her hand. "Lonnie Hodge would have murdered me! Don't ever tell it any different. I can't bear what you went through to save us."

"Can you tell us, Miss Leah," said Toe in an effort at gentleness, "what happened to you and how you came to be here after all these years? Just as you need to know about Lawrence, we need to know your story—if you can tell us."

Leah hesitated, reluctant and subdued but finally trustful enough to open up her heart. The lamplight framed her face and softened it, and her eyes shone as she spoke. We sat listening, mesmerized by her words.

"Rand Saugus led me out of town on that horse, Taffy. He bound my wrists to the saddle horn and took the leader rope. We joined several other raiders as they got away. In the southern hills, we turned to watch the fires that were destroying Lawrence. The sky was black, and smoke was everywhere. Even miles away, ash was raining down on us. I tried to see if they'd torched our home, praying Saugus had kept his word. I never knew for certain, although he claimed as much. 'It was a bargain all the way around,' he said." Leah paused again, ashamed. "And now you're here, Ethan, and I see that he was right."

"It was no bargain for you, Leah." I clenched my fists underneath the table.

"The other raiders mocked and taunted Saugus for bringing a woman out of Lawrence," Leah continued, "but he didn't seem to care. I never once saw Quantrill. I think Saugus purposely stayed clear of him since he'd disobeyed orders. When the men scattered, we joined some who were eastbound for Missouri. No one came after us, at least as far as I could tell. The troop dwindled as the days went by, and each man found his home or hiding place. They all needed to lay low after the raid. Saugus took me to his cousin's house in Blue Ridge, Missouri, and there we stayed for several weeks until the horror over Lawrence began to die.

"I was frightened, terribly so, but there was a woman—the cousin's wife—and several children living at the house, and they were kind to me. Martha, the wife, even railed at Saugus once, telling him he was going to hell for what he'd done to the folks in Lawrence. She told her husband she didn't want a killer in her house. But the husband ignored her, proud of the fame the raiders had acquired, and Martha finally stopped trying. 'You're better off here than out in some cave with Saugus, the Union army after ya,' she said to me one day. But the men ran things and did as they pleased as far as the women were concerned—Saugus most of all.

"I wanted to run away. I thought about it all the time. Saugus was gone a good deal, and I had my chances. But he swore he'd kill me or he'd go back to Lawrence and kill *you*. After a few months, I knew I had a baby coming, and it was no use trying anymore."

Henry and I were silent as Leah spoke. I thought of all the times she'd talked of Zion, of her people's promised land. I remembered everything she had done to prove worthy of the blessing—purity and a sinless life and all—and here she was, starving in a dirty hovel, ideals and dreams all gone. This girl had saved my life—and given hers as much as if that no-good Lonnie Hodge had pulled a knife across her throat.

"I was alone when Grace was born," mused Leah. "We had moved on from the cousin's place by then, and Sargus had joined another raiding party. It was summer, when the Bushwhackers were most on the prowl, and I seldom saw him. I was living in a deserted house outside of Conroy. There was no door or windows. There was no bed, only a few moth-eaten blankets on the floor. I carried water from a nearby creek and tried to keep a fire going. A woman packing kindling to town heard me screaming and stopped to help me. Together we brought my Grace into the world."

"Did Saugus ever see the baby?"

"Oh, yes. He always came back, although sometimes it was several weeks between visits. It's still like that. Grace is four years old and hardly knows her father."

Leah bowed her head. "I dread him coming, Ethan, though he usually brings food and sometimes a little money, which we need desperately. Once he brought a little bonnet and a dress for Gracie. I can hardly stand his grimy hands on her, but at least he treats her with some affection."

"When's he due again?" asked Toe warily.

"It's been two months since we saw him last, and who knows where he is? When the war was at a fever pitch, I figured he'd been killed or wounded if he stayed gone that long. Now, he's a hated vagabond and has to keep one step ahead of bounty hunters, the federal government, and folks from Kansas bent on revenge." Leah's voice turned bitter, her dark eyes dull and lightless. "They deserve the haunted lives their deeds have brought them," she said, "Saugus and all the murderers. They should all hang for what they did, no matter how long it takes." She raised her chin and smiled sadly. "Until then, I live knowing he'll be back someday. He's on the run, but he always seems to remember where we are."

"This time you won't be here when he comes!" I snapped. "You'll never have to look at him again!"

Leah reached up and ran her fingers through my hair. "It's all right, Ethan. What's done is done. You and Addie are safe. That's all that matters."

"It isn't all that matters. I want you to come home, Leah. Come home to Lawrence. Let us take care of you and Grace. You've got to come. Addie misses you. She needs you desperately . . . and so do I."

Leah stood up and turned away. Toe had slid his chair back against the wall, where he listened quietly from the shadows.

Taking the other chair again and moving close to me, Leah spoke gently but with determination as tears stained her cheeks again. "I can't ever go back to Lawrence, Ethan. Don't you understand? The survivors of the massacre will know what happened. They'll see Rand Saugus in Gracie's face, and they'll hate her for what they see. And they'll hate me for surrendering to him. We'd be a constant reminder of their suffering, and you'd be an outcast, too, because of me. I won't do it. I can't, for your sake as well as mine and Gracie's. It hurts me to think I'll never see Addie again, but hopefully she'll understand. Life is full of bitter choices, remember, Ethan? This is another one I have to make."

"What about your faith?" I ventured carefully. "Has Saugus taken that as well?"

Startled, Leah looked at us, and then with great resolve, she spoke decisively. "My circumstances have changed, but not my faith. The Lord has blessed me. He saved you and Addie while others died. He gave me Gracie, a beautiful little daughter, to comfort me and assuage my loneliness. He sent the kindling lady when I cried for help. He helped you find me when I am all but lost to everyone. No, my faith is still strong, Ethan, though my people are far away."

Toe and I laid our bedrolls on the ground that night by Leah's fire. I didn't sleep but talked to Toe until he drifted off. I examined Leah's little hovel of a house and remembered the time I almost spied on her from my mother's closet. She was more physically hardened now—not the buoyant young woman who so entranced me at her bedroom mirror—but I found myself wishing to comfort her. I wanted to protect her as I had that secret night five years before. I wanted to make up somehow for all the terrible things that had happened to her on my account. I remembered what that fellow Joseph Spenser had said about Mormons finding peace and risking everything once they'd been converted. I thought of Leah all that night, and when the sky turned gray in the morning, I was thinking of her still.

"There's only one thing we can do," I told Toe when he woke up. I didn't have to say another word. He knew what I meant and nodded solemnly.

Part Four

Finding Zion

"I'M TAKING YOU TO UTAH, Leah. I owe you more than I can ever pay, but at least I can do that."

She had come out to the fire to cut up some potatoes for our breakfast. We'd laughed and talked for a moment while I washed my face over a bucket and accepted a steaming cup of coffee. Toe had moved behind the shack to dress himself, and I was alone with Leah when I blurted out the words.

She stopped her work and looked at me. "Oh, Ethan," she said, unbelieving.

"Toe and I discussed it, and he wants to come. We're two foot-loose men who want to see the West, and now we got a good reason to do it."

Leah smiled and resumed cutting the potatoes into the frying pan.

"It would be a great adventure, you and me and Gracie and Toe all headed to the Rocky Mountains. We could do it, Leah. There's a fellow we met in St. Louis named Joseph Spenser. He's a Mormon agent crossing Iowa right now with a company of your Saints. We could join up with him. I know we could."

Leah looked up again with more interest. "Do you think that's possible?"

"I know it is! This Spenser was a friendly fellow, anxious to bring everyone he could to Zion. He'd get us there all right."

Pondering this, Leah stirred chopped onions in the pan, and when she looked at me again, it was hard to tell if her tears were from onions or the proposition. "I have no money, Ethan, no supplies. If

I leave my garden, there will be no food. I can't take Grace across a desert as a beggar, dependent on the charity of others for every morsel we eat and every step we take. I can't be that beholden to anyone . . . even you."

"Who said you'd be beholden to anyone?" I knelt down beside her at the fire and slid as close to her as I could get. Taking a money pouch out of my pocket, I tossed it gently in my hands. "My father has never dismissed you from our employ. This money is yours! Our family *owes* you, Leah. We're the ones who are indebted." She dropped the stirring spoon when I reached for her hands. I pressed my forehead against hers as she bowed and lowered her eyes. "I'm not going to leave you in this hovel," I pledged. "I won't leave you alone again."

Leah's tears came in earnest now as she whispered, "Rand will look for us. He'll never let me go."

"Let him look!" I sputtered angrily. "I hope he follows us all the way to Utah so I can put a bullet in his heart!"

She settled me with calming words. "It's all right, Ethan. Rage isn't the answer here. What's done is done. Rand and the others will face justice someday from God. You're not the avenger here. You survived vigilante terror once. I won't put you in harm's way again."

"Then we best leave soon, before Saugus comes back."

★

We bought a pack mule from a hobbled trader in Clifton and tied down the rest of Leah's things in a broken old wagon Saugus had left on the lot, putting our own horses in the harness. There were blankets in the wagon bed for Gracie and almost enough food and water to get us to Iowa. Leah didn't have much to bring—a few keepsakes from the last five years, Gracie's doll, some clothes, a hairbrush and ribbons, pans and hooks, hats, worn shoes, and the books she'd managed to scavenge from somewhere. She had pencils, too, and a little bit of paper. "I had to read and write and teach Grace her letters," she explained. All these things she hurriedly packed along with the store of fruit and vegetables she'd dried.

From a short distance, some of Leah's neighbors watched us curiously as we made our preparations, and Leah was nervous about it. "Keep in the shadows," she told me and Toe. "I don't want them to tell Rand who I left with."

I looked at the two old women sullenly watching us, hands on their hips. "Let them talk," I muttered under my breath, hating the hard, cold glare of strangers. I could see that Leah had found no comfort here from the stonehearted folks surrounding her, and I was almost grateful. There were no neighborly friendships to hold Leah, no ties to sever. It made the going easier, and I lightened up as she became more eager.

"Is this really happening?" she said when the mule was almost weighted down and the wagon ready. "Everything is happening so quickly I can hardly breathe. Now, Ethan, you're sure this Joseph Spenser will let us join his company? You're certain you can find him?"

"He showed me a map."

"I am a baptized member of the Church. Spenser will believe me when I tell him?"

"Of course he will."

"Oh, Ethan, is this possible? Am I really going to Zion after all?"

"Yes, and Gracie too!"

"I can't believe it! I really can't believe it! What will I do there, Ethan? I'm not used to being with other Mormons. What will I do?"

"You'll start a new life, free from . . . all of this."

"Perhaps I could teach school! Or be a children's tutor once again! Oh, I would love that! And I could live among the Saints with Gracie, and she could know what Zion means. Oh, Ethan, can this be happening to me?"

She would talk like this as we packed. But every so often she would look at her frowning neighbors, and the joy would fade for just a moment. "We should hurry," she would say, allowing the dark cloud to pass before her eagerness returned.

★

The farther we got from Clifton and the remnants of Leah's hovel, the better I felt and the more the road ahead seemed like a pathway to the stars. I was ecstatic. I was so filled with warmth and joy I thought my heart would burst. I sat beside Toe on the wagon seat and snapped the lines above the team, keeping them moving north through a green and verdant countryside toward Iowa and Leah's people and her dreams. Leah and Gracie sat in the wagon bed, lying against the quilts, playing games, laughing together. It was almost like Addie was there again and I was leading Taffy through the meadow.

In the evenings we would find a grove of trees or some cove along a river and cook and eat and rest the animals. Leah and Grace slept in the wagon, but sometimes late, after Toe was wrapped in his bedroll on the ground, Leah would join me by the fire and talk quietly about the journey and other things as well. She was not the same young girl who first came to our house with Amos Willard. She had lost the eager radiance she once had, and her bright eyes were often dull and somber.

One night when she seemed extraordinarily pensive, I encouraged her to share her thoughts, and she poured her heart out to me, a nineteen-year-old boy. "Do you remember how I wanted to be worthy of Zion? Do you remember that I promised God a pure life if He'd help me find the way?"

I nodded. There was nothing I remembered more.

"I told you then that you were too young to fully understand what I meant, but I think you did, and surely you do now."

"You are pure, Leah, the purest girl I know."

"You know that's not quite true."

"Yes, it is. You Mormons don't know what virtue means if your God holds the last five years against you."

"God will forgive me, Ethan." She shook her head sadly. "And Zion will accept me. But can I ever again accept myself?" She settled near me, stirring the last embers in the fire. "When I was a girl and first came to Lawrence, I was full of my own self worth. In spite of my poor situation and the fact that, as an orphan, I had my hand out at your door, I felt good about myself. I held fast to my principles. I had studied and become well versed in the way of books. I had esteem and felt I was worth something. The last five years have taken that away, Ethan. The way I've been treated, the pig sties I've been dragged through, the absence of anyone who shared my beliefs—I'm different than I was five years ago. My sense of my own virtue was taken from me, and I don't know if I'll ever get it back."

"You told me you still had your faith." Her words pained me. "You told me that!"

"I still believe in God and Zion," she conceded, "just not so much in myself. Something happens to a person when her sense of worth diminishes. It's like losing part of your soul and with it the reason to keep striving. If it weren't for Grace . . ."

"That's all in your mind, Leah. You're as good and virtuous as you've always been. Don't talk like this."

She wearily receded into silence, and I was sorry I hadn't been more understanding. She had so much to overcome.

★

We were well into Iowa when the first shots struck the wagon and sent all of us dashing for cover. Leah screamed and pulled Grace under her in the wagon, but they were still so exposed that Toe and I had to get them out of there before we could hide ourselves. Bullets were flying all around, splintering the sides of the wagon and ringing off the iron wheels. Toe let off several rounds with his rifle while I wrestled Leah and Grace out of the wagon and down into the grass along the edge of a gully. We had no idea where the shots were coming from. Toe fired blindly to cover us. Leaving Leah with her crying child, I rushed to the top of the incline to help Toe.

At that moment I saw a man on the road above, swinging his horse around, firing a pistol into the sky, and galloping toward a stand of trees that partially concealed him.

"You think you can take my woman, do ya?" he shouted from behind the trees. "You think you can take my family?" His voice rang again with anger. "I don't know who you are, but you're dead men if you think you can steal what's mine!"

We lay silent, listening to his rant. I looked across at Toe and saw a soft grin slip across his face. "Looks like Rand Saugus has caught up with us," he whispered. "I wonder if Bobbie is watchin'."

Toe moved quietly down the gully, planning to come up on Saugus from the other side. I yelled back as a diversion, knowing Saugus wouldn't give a hoot or holler what I said. "Leah's leaving by her own choice," I shouted. "You got nothing to say about it!"

"Devil if I don't!" cried Saugus.

"You're a thief and a murderer, and Leah wants no part of you. The federal officers will take you, though, and hang you high for what you did."

"Hah!" thundered Saugus. "Just let 'em try!"

I heard a belch of gunfire, mostly coming from where Toe should be by now. There were one or two shots returned, popping quickly. Then I heard thrashing through the trees followed by the hoofbeats of a horse in full gallop, gaining distance.

Toe came out of the trees with his rifle and walked toward me, disappointed but unharmed. "It was like trying to flush a pheasant," he said. "I needed a scattergun to do the job. I missed 'im with the rifle. Scared 'im though. Sent 'im runnin'." Toe put his fingers to his lips and then raised his arm to heaven. "Next time, Bobbie boy. Next time."

Leah was devastated. "Oh, I'm sorry! I'm so sorry! He could have killed you," she sobbed, "and it's all my fault!" She shook her head over and over as if in shock. "I don't know how he found us. He's been gone so long, and now this. Maybe I'm destined to be miserable, trapped by my own bitter deeds. Oh, I should never have let you bring me along. He won't rest."

Toe was the first to reply. "I'm glad he found us," he declared with more fire on his tongue than I'd ever heard from him. "Because that means we found *him*, Miss Leah, and that's what I vowed to do."

From then on we traveled with a wary eye, Toe on guard with his rifle ready while I drove the team, and then me spelling him from time to time. We'd found the main trail through southern Iowa and saw signs of the Mormon presence along the way—wildflowers that previous bands had planted, camping spots with evidence of large wagons circling while their animals grazed, travelers who told us that Spenser and his company weren't too far ahead of us. At one place we even came across a tattered copy of the Book of Mormon, overlooked and left there in the dust. Leah was ecstatic at the find.

"I left mine behind in Lawrence," she said, "and have never found another until now." She reverently thumbed through the pages. "Now I can read some of the verses to Gracie as I used to do to you."

"Tell her the story of Nephi on the ship and how his faith saved his people from the storm," I suggested, and Leah smiled, remembering.

We saw no more of Saugus once we found the main migration trail. It was well traveled, with wagons and carriages and horses often passing us both ways, and there was a measure of safety in the numbers, although we never failed to remain alert. In towns and villages along the way were blacksmith shops and carters and wheelwrights, folks who catered to the traffic. There were ox traders as well and canvas menders and medicine drummers and all kinds of merchants looking to make a dollar from the slow migration.

With our money, we had no trouble becoming well supplied, our little wagon well enough prepared. I considered acquiring a Conestoga wagon—a regular prairie schooner with a large white cover and comfortable springs—but I wasn't sure what kind of outfits Spenser's company would have or how we would blend in, so I waited, hoping our little buckboard would catch up before we needed to make a change.

The heat of June beat down on us and left us sticky and foul by each day's end. The dust billowed up on breezy afternoons and left sand in our clothes and grit on our sweaty faces. Leah had her broad straw hat and one for Gracie too, but when the dry wind whipped about, the hats didn't do much good. Our cheeks were brown and burned. Toe's thickening whiskers offered some protection, as did mine, but Leah's face grew dark in the summer sun, and Grace, who was fairer skinned, blistered in places. Leah found some aloe plants and used the oil from the pods to soothe her daughter's nose and cheeks. She offered me and Toe some. I wanted to help her apply the salve to her own dry skin, but she laughed and told me my fingers were too rough.

★

We reached the Missouri River at Council Bluffs by the last week of the month and crossed over to Nebraska on ferry barges that accommodated the wagon, our animals, and four weary passengers looking somewhat dazedly at more of the same green prairie we'd found in Iowa.

I watched Leah bubble with enthusiasm as we drove through this town where she had lived. She pointed out her school, her neighborhood, and a Christian church whose pastor had allowed the tiny Mormon congregation to meet on Sunday evenings once the regular services were over.

"I miss our little branch," Leah said. "I gained my testimony of the Restoration there and a firm foundation in our scriptures and theology. They were a faithful group and kind in every way."

After being ferried across the river, we moved north to Florence and the place the Saints called Winter Quarters. The cemetery was the largest remaining piece of the settlement, but a few cabins still stood where Leah had once played as a child. Several Mormons were still there, stationed at this established crossroads to provide support and encouragement for the converts who were still pouring out of Europe and doggedly marching to Zion and the promised land. It was hard to believe I was now one of them, if in name only. I had never been particularly interested in religion before Leah came along, and after the tragedy at Lawrence, I was ready to give up on God altogether. But Leah's continued devotion touched me. I was curious about Zion, this place of refuge for so many, this City on a Hill that thousands sacrificed so much to reach. It became a beacon to me simply because that's what it was to Leah. Having seen my hometown destroyed, I began to yearn for solace in a holy and protected place.

We asked about Joseph Spenser and were told he was some miles ahead. "The companies try to reach Independence Rock by the Fourth of July," said one old codger. "Then they're pretty sure they can make the Valley before the snow flies. That's what they hope for, anyway."

Chapter Two

NEBRASKA TURNED OUT TO BE even more desolate than Iowa. It was still green along the riverbeds, and elm and locust trees still lined the creeks and meadows. But the verdant farms soon became less frequent, and large swaths of prairie grass replaced the abundant fields of corn and wheat we first encountered. It was an isolated country with a lonely sod house occasionally appearing on some deserted acreage. There were few trees for lumber, so sod was the material of necessity in spite of the wind that gnawed at it and the rain that turned it soft. The sky caught your attention because it was so wide and high, its span stretching like a dome over all we could see.

Near the Platte River, at a little town called Jolley, the dome cracked like a shattered mirror, and rain seeped through the edges in violent bursts that kept us huddled in an abandoned stable for two full days. The shack was built against a hillock and had only one entry, but it was roomy enough to offer shelter for us and our horses. We kept busy piling the straw high enough to keep it above the soggy floor and dry enough for sleeping, and we'd dropped our guard as far as Saugus was concerned. Following the trail where Spenser and his party had passed just days before, we figured to see their wagons within the week. The rain was stalling us, but it was likely impeding Spenser too, so we could still close the gap in good time once the storm was over.

We plugged the stable's many leaks with some of our extra quilts and nestled Gracie in a warm, protected corner full of straw. The little girl seemed to have a growing curiosity about Toe and had taken a liking to him. The first night in the stable, while the rain drummed on the roof, lightning lit up the cracks and crevices, and our one lantern added its flame, Leah and I watched Toe play finger games with Gracie as they sat together in the straw.

Mesmerized by Toe's facile hands as he turned a penny through his fingers and made it disappear, Gracie suddenly asked with childlike wonder, "Why is your skin burned like that? Were you in the sun too long?"

Toe grinned and winked in our direction. "No, I wasn't burned, child. I was born this way. Some folks are, ya know."

"Why?" said Gracie innocently.

"Oh, it's a gift from God," laughed Toe. "He knew the world would be one dull place if folks all looked alike."

"It's nice," declared the little girl, assessing Toe's dark hand.

"Yes, it is," said Toe, rubbing his thumb against his skin. "And that's a lesson your ma taught me when I was just a boy."

"How did she do that?"

"She put me in a story play where we acted out the parts."

"The one where you played a girl!" giggled Gracie, dimpling.

"Yeah, that's the one!" Toe smiled. "Except the play was really about a colored man like me. It told his story. In that way, it told my story too, so I was proud to be just like him, right down to the color of my skin." Toe looked at Leah listening nearby. "Your ma did that for me." He gently patted Gracie's head as he smiled at her mother.

I've always treasured that night in the stable. In some ways it was like that last summer evening on our porch at home, just before the massacre. Bobbie wasn't with us this time, and Grace had taken Addie's place, but the four of us were "connected" again in warmth and reverie, and just as it was in Lawrence, things would be different in the morning.

On that second night, when Gracie had been put to bed and was covered and cozy in the straw, a clap of thunder jarred us, and I thought the roof was falling in. But it wasn't thunder. It was gunfire, rapid and constant, splitting through the beams and boards of the leaky stable. Toe and I grabbed our rifles, while Leah flew toward Grace, holding the girl tightly as she began to cry.

Peering cautiously through the rain-soaked cracks of the shelter, I saw Rand Saugus standing ten yards from our door and glowing like the devil's angel each time the lightning struck. With no concern for aim, he was randomly firing two different weapons, a pistol and a shotgun, keeping one or the other smoking as he paused to reload. Between shots he raged like a mad man, dancing and shouting in the rain. "I've got you now! I've found all of you! You send out what's mine, or I'll burn that shack and everything that's in it! I swear I will!"

I would have killed Saugus where he stood, but before I found my rifle and a place to aim, he had moved back into the shadows behind our wagon, and I'd missed my chance. It was the same for Toe, who was dodging incoming rounds like I was and couldn't get a level shot.

Saugus's threat to burn us out was an idle one. The rain had drenched the stable and continued to come down, so a fire was impossible. Still, the anger in his voice was real. The bullets whined and thudded against our shelter, and I feared for Leah's sanity as she and Gracie clung together, trembling at every sound.

All that night we listened to Saugus taunting us, his violent, drunken shrieks piercing the storm. By dawn the rain had ceased, but we waited long into the morning before we tried to make a move. Muddy swill puddles filled every hole around the shelter, and some had seeped inside. We'd kept watch through the gaps between the slats, and when all we heard was the leaking and dripping from the roof, Toe and I ventured toward the wooden door. The second we creaked it open, a fusillade sent us backward to the floor. The charge from the rifle scattered buckshot up and down the door jamb, splintering the edges and ringing off the rusty hinges.

"Poke your nose out again, and I'll blow it off!" bellowed Saugus from behind the wagon. "The devil never sleeps, ya know. You won't catch me nappin'!"

"What do you want, Saugus? You expect to hold us here all day?"

"You know what I want, my woman and my girl. You send 'em on out before I torch the shed."

"You're good at burning things and threatening women and children, ain't you Saugus?" I yelled out, firing an angry shot through the slats. Trouble was, I couldn't see Saugus well enough to fix my aim. My bullet ripped through the spokes of the left wagon wheel, sending sparks jumping as it struck and drawing a shriek from the man I was aiming for.

"Yer all trapped like chickens in a slaughterhouse!" he screamed. "There's no help for you on this prairie. Best give up what's mine and be on yer way!"

Behind me Leah hung her head, held on to Grace, and fought back tears. She blamed herself for our trouble, and the more I tried to reason with her, the more miserable she became.

"I'd walk out that door now if it weren't for Grace. I did it once to save you, Ethan, and I'd do it now. But you've given Gracie hope, even if mine is all but lost. I won't surrender to that man again."

"And I wouldn't let you," I whispered to her.

★

All that day we waited, keeping an eye on Saugus's every move. There was nothing gained by firing our guns, no hope for a truce. I wouldn't let Leah near the door to plead for one. Occasionally, shots rang out from behind the wagon, and Saugus would curse and whine, but by late afternoon he'd turned ominously quiet. The prairie sun was brasslike after the rain stopped, the heat thick and humid, which only added to the tension.

"Maybe he's finally sleepin'," Toe muttered as we squinted through the creases, trigger ready. "He was blastin' at us all night long and most of today. How much longer can he last?"

We were all in a bad way. Toe and I had traded off guard duty with each other, catching a little rest from constant watch although no real sleep. Grace had cried herself tired and dozed fitfully in her mother's arms for a while, but I never once saw Leah shut her eyes. Now Grace was awake again, begging to "go home."

It came to me again, the fear and panic of the priest hole all those years before, being in a tight place, unable to move or free myself, with danger waiting if I did. There's a phobia connected with tight places, and the priest hole made me prone to that. The little stable was no priest hole, but we were trapped in a small space, and I fought a similar wave of desperation. It helped to look at Leah, to know this time she was with me. I was glad that this time I stood between her and Saugus rather than the other way around.

Suddenly, the silence outside ended. Saugus began shouting again. But his tone had changed, and now he sounded pathetic and wretched. "Leah!" he cried miserably. "Leaaah!" He fired his gun into the air every time he said her name, and then he began moaning about the "blood of Lawrence" haunting him and the hangman coming. Next he'd chant angrily, promising revenge on everyone who'd taken what was his—from his property in Lawrence to his freedom and his pride. "Leah," he shrieked at last, "you won't get away from me! I'm dead and done, but so are you. I'll never let you go!"

To this day I don't know how Saugus started the fire in the wagon. It must have been full of rainwater, its contents too wet and soggy for any match. Maybe he found enough dry straw underneath the boxes. Maybe he was able to pour enough gunpowder around to catch a light. I never saw any flames, but suddenly white smoke was rising from the wagon, and soon it was engulfed, rainwater and all, belching like a locomotive whistling steam. From where the wagon stood to our only door was a slight decline of about ten yards, and Saugus shoved the smoking cart down that slope, lifting the tongue and guiding its course until it smashed headlong into our shelter, blocking the entrance and sending smoke into every corner of the shack. Then a shot rang out, a final punctuation to a desperate act. Rand Saugus lay dead at the far side of the wagon, a victim of his own pistol and his own evil, which was not yet at an end.

The wagon was too damp to burn quickly, and no flames reached our wooden shelter, but the smoke, white and billowing from the bed, was just as lethal. Sucked in through every crease, it began to fill the room, driving Leah and Gracie to the ground searching for breath. Toe and I put our shoulders to the door, pushing with all our strength, but the wagon was wedged awkwardly against the frame. The harder we pushed, the tighter the wedge. We pounded on the slats of the hut with our rifle butts and managed to splinter away enough to help us breathe, but as the air poured through so did the smoke with its acrid smell and its falling ash. I thought of Mayor Collamore dying in his well in Lawrence, not from a raider's bullet but from suffocation as his house burned next to his hiding place. In a panic I pounded away at the walls of the shelter with renewed vigor, determined not to die like that with safety just a foot away.

But it was of little use. The stable was a dugout, surrounded by rock on three sides. The only escape lay in the front, but the wagon smoldered there and blocked the door. Even the roof was a smoking trap, rain-drenched though it was. Of course, Toe and I would not give up. We continued to push and beat and splinter the slats with our rifles. My eyes were burning, and my nostrils and lungs were filling with smoke, but I couldn't stop. Leah was wrapped around Gracie on the ground, barely visible. I could hear her praying with all her heart. "O Heavenly Father, help us. O Heavenly Father, save my child. O Heavenly Father, please remember me."

Just then, we heard voices from outside, loud voices. "Is anybody there? Is there life in the dugout? Answer if you can!"

As Toe and I began to call back frantically, we heard the sound of the wagon being pushed and knocked away from the door. Soon hammers and gun butts were breaking through the wedge, and light and air were mixing with the smoke, allowing us to breathe.

One by one our rescuers pulled us through the frame to safety.

It was the big blond Mormon, Joseph Spenser, who hovered over me as I coughed and wheezed and rubbed my eyes.

"Hah! It's the boy from Lawrence, Ethan Pace," he roared, "and his good friend Mr. Kettle! Never thought I'd see you two again!" Spenser and three companions had us spread out on the ground upwind from the smoke, helping us all catch our breath. "What're ya doin' out here in Nebraska, Ethan? You were bound for Cole County, last I knew."

"We were lookin' for you, Spenser," I sputtered gratefully. "I'm glad you found us first."

Chapter Three

"WE'RE ONLY A COUPLE MILES yonder," said Spenser as we sat about that evening, breathing easy once again and soot cleaned from our faces. "We saw the smoke and remembered this little shelter we'd passed two days ago. I was gonna let it be, thinking it was just a campfire someone built too tall, but something prodded me to ride back and take a look, and I'm glad we did." He pondered Leah, smeared with soot and sorrow. "I reckon it was your prayin' that brought me," he said, trying to draw a smile from her. "You're closer to the Lord than these two fellas. That's my guess."

Leah didn't smile. She was too filled with weariness and guilt. But she raised her chin toward Joseph Spenser. "I'm grateful to you, sir, from the bottom of my heart."

We buried Rand Saugus there by the smoldering shelter, the remnant of the chaos he had caused. Leah and Gracie watched us from a few yards off and didn't go near the grave. I thought Leah might speak some final words, but she looked on grimly until we finished, never even whispering to Grace. I thought of all the folks who'd died that day in Lawrence. Old George Kreiger, Louis Carpenter, Mr. Fitch, Reverend Snyder, Mayor Collamore, Mr. Williamson, Mr. Hay, and a score of others I personally knew. Mostly I thought of my friend Bobbie Martin, and I know Toe was thinking of him too. This wasn't William Clarke Quantrill we were burying. It wasn't Bloody Bill Anderson either. But it was good enough. Saugus had taken his own life, driven to it by the demons in his past, and it was fitting after all the evil he had done.

"How was it you were so nearby?" I asked Spenser, still wondering at our good fortune. "We figured you were almost to Wyoming. Independence Rock by July 4, isn't that what you Mormons calculate?"

"*These* Mormons are a bunch of tortoises!" Spenser laughed. "Slower than cold tar." He looked about at the damage, the grave we had just filled, and the lives he and his friends had saved. "From broken wagon wheels to birthin' babies, I've had more trouble with this outfit than any I've ever brought across the prairie. One thing or another, it seems like something was always holding us up." He winked in my direction. "You just never know what it's gonna be."

Saugus had run our animals off, and it had taken some time to round them up. Most of our goods had been destroyed or damaged in the smoke and fire, but we packed what remained on the mule and set out for Spenser's company the following day. The men provided food and water and took special care with Gracie, who clung to Leah in a state of shock. By and by, Toe made her laugh again by dotting her cheeks and the end of her little nose with soot and showing her face in a pocket mirror. The clownlike image worked its wonders. Gracie giggled at herself and finally let Toe carry her, giving Leah some relief.

I was worried about Leah. Her shoulders sagged, and she seldom spoke or smiled. She rode behind me once we'd found my horse, and I felt warm and protective with her arms around my waist. When she laid her head wearily on my shoulder, I was never more content. But Leah was burdened by a misery I couldn't grasp. Our very real brush with death, the shock of Saugus's violence—all were part of it. But I sensed something else as well.

I still have faith in God, she'd told us back in Iowa, *but not so much in myself.* And there were more of Leah's words that still whispered to me. *My sense of my own virtue has been taken from me*, she'd said. *I don't know if I'll ever get it back.*

★

If there was ever a group of people to remind Leah of the gospel that she cherished, it was the little company of Saints we joined under the leadership of Joseph Spenser. These folks, most of them of strong character but not rich in the ways of the world, accepted all of us into their caravan with Christlike sympathy. They didn't seem to care that Toe was colored or that Leah had a child but no husband or that I looked like a roustabout trying to hitch a free ride to the West. They heard our story and took us in. We were welcome at their fire. They were immigrants—some from Great Britain, some from Scandinavia—full of hope and wonder as they headed toward Zion. I was soon caught up in the industrious, faithful spirit they possessed.

These were families with children Gracie's age and teenage boys and babies newly born. There were dutiful young girls who helped their mothers with the cooking and able fathers trying to spare their wives the worst of the labor as they all crossed the rugged country, watching a foreign, unfamiliar land spread out before them. They prayed night and day. Oh, how these people prayed! It was as if they recognized all of their vast inadequacies, knew they had no business making a 1,300-mile trek, and would survive it only by the grace of God. They prayed mightily for that grace and found it in the common bond of love and faith they shared.

Although I could understand and speak to the English folks better, I liked the Scandinavians best. Most of them were from Norway. They were a little less stiff than the English, and their communication with me consisted of a lot of friendly *ja, ja, ja*'s coupled with appreciative nods. I loved their kindness and their willingness to give anything they could to help us, though they had so little themselves. Their language interested me. I noticed they mingled together, feeling more comfortable with those who could speak their native language but still anxious to be part of the larger group. The prayers and songs brought them together, and when Joseph Spenser spoke every night at a sort of group devotional, they listened eagerly to whispered interpretations from those who could translate.

We sang hymns together most nights, and even the Norwegians knew a favorite one by rote. It was called "Come, Come, Ye Saints," and there was a line in it that said, "And should we die before our journey's through, happy day! All is well!" I thought of the folks in Lawrence who had died long before their earthly journey should have ended. I hoped all was well with them, and as I sang with these faithful people on the plains, I got the feeling that it was.

★

When we reached Wyoming, the land became even more bleak and foreboding. The occasional patches of Nebraska sunflowers were now replaced by tufts of sagebrush and dry expanses of dust and sand. Streambeds shrank, windstorms multiplied, and our world became hot and blistered and gritty. We were behind schedule, and it was the last week in July before we made Independence Rock, a giant boulder on the prairie where dozens before us had carved their initials. Toe and I used a knife to scratch ours in the stone, but I felt a little guilty doing it. I wasn't a Mormon and didn't feel quite right placing my mark not far from Brigham Young's.

Later, we stood at the top of the great boulder and looked back where we had come from and forward into the western sun at the road we had yet to travel. I turned to Joseph Spenser with solemn wonder. "Why do they do it?" I asked him plaintively. "Why do they come all this way? Why do they risk all they have for Zion?"

"You and Toe come by my fire some night," said Spenser, "and I'll tell ya why."

And so we did.

Joseph Spenser taught Toe and me the gospel of Jesus Christ, the gospel of the Restoration. He taught us of the Atonement and of the great plan, established in the heavens before the world was. Knowing of our tragic history in Lawrence, Spenser taught us the principle of restitution and how true forgiveness is a balm for the victim even as the violator is chastened. He taught us of continuing revelation and the power of the Holy Ghost. Over several nights we read the Book of Mormon together and prayed about its message, and Spenser laid his hands on both of us and blessed us with his priesthood and authority.

Toe and I were baptized in the Sweetwater River on an August day that was hot and dry, without a breath of air. The sky above us was like crystal—blue and clear and full of light. The entire company of immigrants stood by as Spenser performed the ordinance for both of us. Leah was there with Gracie, smiling over the event and singing like an angel as we all celebrated the sacred occasion with speeches, love, and handshakes.

I did feel like a new man once the ordinance was over. I felt clean and pure in the eyes of God, ready to meet the world with a new spirit of peace. I began to see why these covenants meant so much to Leah even as an orphan girl in a lonely Kansas town. I began to understand the lure of Zion, the dream of living with God's people in a promised land protected from the evil of the world. I was becoming one of them.

As the rugged miles passed, however, there was something that gnawed at me, leaving my new rapture somewhat incomplete. Joseph Spenser was falling in love with Leah, and there was nothing I could do but watch.

Of course it was bound to happen. Leah was still as lovely as an angel in spite of all her troubles—or perhaps because of them, in Spenser's way of thinking. He had rescued her, a lady in distress, and perhaps saw destiny's hand in the circumstances. He could forge ahead with confidence, being a handsome, broad-shouldered elder of the Church with a firm foundation in the gospel Leah loved. There was no other unmarried man in the train with those qualities. The path to Leah's heart was open for Spenser if he chose to take it, and much to my annoyance, it appeared he would.

Spenser wasn't bold in his courtship of Leah. We never saw him single her out at any of the gatherings. He never called on her to pray or speak or do anything to give particular notice. Sometimes on a calm, warm evening, the Norwegians would play their harmonicas and dance. Swen Hanson had a violin, and Olag Anderson, a drum. Folks would skip about to the rhythm they created and sometimes pair off for the slower tunes. Spenser never asked Leah to dance or to join in the sing-along when he led the chorus. He still left her and Gracie's primary care to us. Toe and I found wood for her fire, made sure her water bucket was full, and ate in her circle. Though she gratefully shared the Melton family's wagon, Leah made her own meals and always ate with us. Spenser, who took his captain's duties very seriously, usually joined some family for supper, but he never lingered long with any circle and gave himself no extra time for leisure and common pleasure.

Still, I would occasionally notice him looking wistfully at Leah. His eyes would follow her about the camp when he thought no one was watching. Once I surprised them as I came around the Melton wagon looking for the water pot. Spenser had caught Leah alone and stopped to talk to her. I embarrassed him by appearing suddenly, I think, though Leah didn't seem to mind.

"Howdy, Ethan," he said kindly, quick to touch his hat. "I was looking for you and figured Leah might know where you were."

I didn't believe that for a minute.

Another time when Leah stumbled in the wagon ruts and was in some danger of being kicked or trampled over by the oxen, Spenser hurried to the scene. She wasn't hurt much—skinned knees and elbows, a bruised cheekbone—but I saw terror in Spenser's eyes when he came up and saw Leah on the ground. We had stopped the oncoming team, and Toe held them while I went to help.

She'd tripped and fallen headlong against the hardened ruts, but she was embarrassed about anyone fussing over her. She even laughed self-consciously when I tried to lift her. "Oh, Ethan, let me lie here for a minute till I catch my breath. You know I only stumbled so I could take a little rest."

"Leah!" yelled Spenser in alarm. It was the first time I'd ever heard him use her first name, and I was bitten by it. He pushed in, helped Leah to her feet, and made her lean on him as he took her to the wagon where the salves and medicines were kept. I suppose he fussed over her there too, although there was a woman in that wagon who probably did the doctoring. Leah was up and around by evening with no harm done, but Spenser wouldn't take his eyes off her, and I could tell that he was thoroughly smitten.

Joby Crockett came to mind as I watched all of this unfold. I remembered getting hot down to my hands over Crockett, hating him with adolescent petulance and scorn. Spenser was different. He wasn't the smooth and seductive Romeo that Crockett had been. Spenser had been good to us. He'd saved our lives. He'd taught me and Toe the gospel and baptized us. He was a strong and upright Mormon, as good for Leah as anyone could be. But *I* was different too. I was no longer that teenaged pup caught up in an impossible infatuation. I was a man now and ready to fight for what I wanted. And Joseph Spenser or not, there was nothing I wanted more than Leah.

I found myself searching for an opportunity to be alone with her, to talk to her straight about my feelings. If Spenser was preparing to make his bid, I didn't want to be left flat-footed. I loved Leah too, and

I'd loved her longer. Our history gave me a corner on her affections and an edge in this new rivalry. At least I told myself as much. But the anxiety nearly killed me as I waited for the proper moment. Gracie was usually underfoot. Toe was often nearby. Leah had become friendly with several women in the camp, and seldom was there a day without a visit from two or three of them, chattering endlessly about the weather or their children or their voyage across the ocean.

Then one day Leah and I went berry picking along a low ridge where wild current and huckleberry bushes were flourishing. We took baskets and combed the foliage, leaving Gracie playing with Sister Foster's children and Toe greasing the wagon axles. Spenser had ordered an early halt that day, concerned about the oxen as the incline of the land grew sharper. We had crossed through South Pass and could see the mountain ranges looming to the west of us. Zion waited just beyond those rugged peaks, and the hardest part of the journey lay ahead. We were eager and anxious, all at once, with so much promise and so much challenge still ahead.

I had a similar feeling about following Leah into the huckleberry bushes with our baskets. My grief and ecstasy over her were coming to a crossing point.

"Oh, Ethan," said Leah as we found great clusters of the fruit on one bush and then another, "do you remember when we used to do this out at the Carpenter place? Louis and Mary had such beautiful vines and shrubs that summer. I wonder . . . if Mary has been able to keep them up." She paused then and dropped her eyes. In spite of finding Zion, Lawrence and the war were clearly never far from Leah's mind.

She looked up at me rather suddenly and with sorrow in her face. "We've come through a lot together, haven't we? But we're almost there. We're almost home." She looked about at the sky and prairie behind us and the highland ridges before us. Pausing to tweak my cheek, she added, "I'm glad Zion can be a refuge for you after all you've suffered. You survivors of the Lawrence tragedy deserve a new beginning more than anyone."

"You're the one that's suffered," I said quickly, "but I aim to change all that for you and for Gracie too."

"You already have, Ethan, in every way."

"All but one," I stuttered, nearly losing my resolve.

"What do you mean?" Leah was concentrating on the berries she was picking and spoke offhandedly.

"Marriage for you?" I said cautiously. "Will Zion offer that?"

Leah stopped her picking and looked aimlessly into her basket. "I don't think so. I have Gracie now, and that will be enough. I can't see any man really loving me after . . . all that's happened."

"Joseph Spenser loves you," I blurted out.

"Joseph Spenser?" She was genuinely surprised. "No, that's silly."

"I've seen how he looks at you. He wants to kiss you, and he can hardly keep his hands off you whenever he's around."

"Surely, you're joking!"

"Why wouldn't he love you? Every man I know has been enchanted with you. Why wouldn't he feel the same?"

"Oh, Ethan," Leah cried, dropping her basket and turning solemn, "I have a poor history with men who've wanted to love me. Joby Crockett was a fine boy, and I led him on, letting him kiss me when I shouldn't have. It made him want and expect more from me than I could give, and it ruined our romance in the end."

"Joby Crockett! That swellhead? How can you blame yourself for what he did?" I was angry now and gripped Leah's shoulders in both hands. "I suppose you blame yourself for Saugus too and what he did to you!" Tears came to my eyes as I held her there. "You've got to give up the guilt. You've got to love yourself again, for I always have."

She slowly raised her head to look at me, wonder glowing in her eyes. "What are you talking about, Ethan?"

"I love you, Leah. I always have, and I always will. It was infatuation once. I was a kid and didn't know what it meant to feel this much. But now I do, and I swear I love you in every way a man can love a woman, as a friend, a brother, and a fellow Mormon. Now, I want to be a husband too and cherish you forever."

Leah pushed me away ever so slightly. A shadow of alarm covered her face. "Ethan . . . I don't know what . . . I don't know what I did to make you think . . ." She was miserably grasping for words. "Ethan, you're nineteen years old. I'm nearly twenty-five. I have a child. It wouldn't be right for us to . . ."

"Why wouldn't it be right?" I pleaded desperately. "I'm a man now, Leah, a grown man, a Mormon, like you, baptized and bound for Zion."

"I hope you didn't do that for me," she answered miserably. "I hope you did it for yourself."

"I did it for both of us. I love you, Leah. I've loved you since the day you first came to our house with Amos Willard carrying your trunk." I tried to smile. "You cast a spell on me, and I've never quite recovered."

I meant to be romantic and lighthearted, but Leah took it differently. "I'm so sorry, Ethan. Oh, I'm so sorry. You were just a boy, and I had no right to make you think . . . God forgive me if I toyed with your affections."

"What? Leah, you did nothing wrong. *You saved my life*, for heaven's sake! You saved Addie and me by putting us in the priest hole! You sacrificed yourself for us!"

"And you've brought me to Zion," she returned soberly. "You owe me nothing more, certainly not a marriage. I'm 'used goods,' Ethan. Life has more to offer you than that."

"Don't talk that way."

Tears welled in her eyes, but she remained stiff and resolute. "If you've grown up, Ethan, so have I. That terrible day at Lawrence changed us both. Saugus forced me to go with him, it's true, but don't you suppose there were times in all those years that I could have left, that I could have walked away from him? He was gone for weeks at a time. I could have escaped. I was frightened, sure. I was scared to death, especially after I had Gracie. But I could have done it. I could have been as brave as Eliza carrying her baby through that icy river while the hound dogs chased her. Remember that? But it was just a story. It was a parlor game we played. In reality, I couldn't do it. I taught you and Addie faith and courage that I didn't have myself. I promised God a moral life, and I broke that promise, Ethan. Every time Saugus came back again, I broke that promise. God, in His mercy, is bringing me to Zion, but for Gracie's sake, not mine."

Oh, Leah. I took hold of her shoulders, frightened now and determined to tell her again that she'd done nothing wrong, that I loved her innocently and with every fiber of my soul. But she stiffened and pulled away.

"Please don't touch me, Ethan. Don't ever touch me again. I love you . . . but I can't *love* you, not like that. Do you understand?" She turned and walked decisively down the path toward camp with her basket full of berries and her dark head bowed. She never once looked back as I painfully watched her go.

★

The pall cast over me after that was hard to hide. For the remainder of the long journey, as we climbed through the sagebrush hills and looked up in awe at the rising peaks, I saw hardly anything of Leah. She did her best to avoid me, sticking close to the Meltons when she worked or slept. She and Grace joined them for evening meals, which used to be shared with me and Toe. During morning prayers, Leah refused to look at me and went about her chores immediately with the other women, never giving me a chance to catch her alone or speak to her again. Gracie still bubbled whenever she saw Toe and me, and she would often run into my arms or let Toe hoist her on his shoulder for a "walk around," but Leah never let Grace "bother" us too long.

"Come, Grace," she'd say, "come play with the other little girls. The men have work to do. You mustn't be in the way." Grace would dutifully join her mother and the other children.

I couldn't help noticing that Leah kept a bit of distance between herself and Spenser too. She used the other women as a shield, always placing herself in the middle of a group or keeping up a rolling conversation with friends instead of retreating to some corner where Spenser might come along. I think it irritated him, for he became more tense and anxious as we pushed closer to the Valley. Usually mild mannered and in complete control, he was sharper with the animals, impatient with the Norwegians, and eager to rid himself of any nagging annoyance, large or small. "These last miles are the worst part of the trek," he told me. "A team can lose its footing easy on these narrow stretches. Going down is worse. A wagon's brakes give out, and you have the whole load slamming into the outfit out in front or rumbling down the hill, wheels over bed springs, and crushing everything inside. We'll cut some logs and chain them on as weights," he added, "but it makes me nervous every time."

Spenser was nervous all right, but I guessed there was more to it than just the wagon brakes.

As for me, my whole world had ended. My heart still pounded whenever I saw Leah, even from a distance. I thought about her all the time and wished I could go back to those days at Lawrence when we used to ride our horses up to Harrow Road or throw snowballs in the winter. I remembered the day Leah came to Detmer's Grove and called us heroes for building that ladder up the wall and keeping watch. I imagined Louis and Mary Carpenter coming to call and how happy Leah was when she was with them. I even remembered the night we saw Leah kissing Joby Crockett out by the style and how annoyed I was about it. I knew I'd be willing to relive those moments if only Leah was herself again. Most of all, I remembered the night I had been tempted to spy on Leah through the splinter creases in the closet. Heck, I was the one who had sinned, not Leah. Why was she the one with all the guilt?

Toe sensed my gloom for several days before he said anything. Then one night, as he stirred the coals at our fire, he spoke about it. "Are you staying on, once we get there, Eth?" he asked. "Will it be Zion for you, then, if Leah's not a part of things?"

"She'll always be a part of *me* if I leave or stay."

"Then it's prob'ly better not to keep too close. She'll go on without you, Eth, and it'll tear yer heart out. We've kept the faith and brought Leah out of slavery to the promised land. It's best we go back to Lawrence now and be part of what we left behind."

I looked up at him across the fire pit, a black man who'd trekked across the prairie for his friends. "Is that what you'll do, Toe? Go back to Lawrence? You're a Mormon now, you know, officially baptized and worthy of comin' to Zion."

"I heard Miss Leah say once that Zion is in the heart. It's anywhere God calls ya. It's wherever good folks go and feel at home. For me, that's Lawrence. The town paid a bloody price in the war for siding with folks like me. I owe 'em somethin'—the gospel maybe or just a helpin' hand." He paused and looked away, the fire's gleam still in his eyes. "Bobbie's restin' peaceful now. Leah's on her way to Zion. Those things are taken care of. So I reckon I'll go home."

"Spenser says we'll top that next hill and see great Salt Lake City in the morning. You're not going to leave until you've actually laid eyes on the place?!"

"We should both turn tail and gallop right out of here in the morning," Toe laughed warmly, "before the sight of 'beautiful Zion' and Leah's joy at finally gettin' there becomes too much for you to take."

"I'm not leaving, Toe. I'll live in Leah's shadow until she comes to see me different than she does. I lost her once. I'm not leaving her again."

"She's already gone, Ethan. She's lost to you the same as if you'd never found her. Best let it be."

Chapter Four

THE MOUNTAIN WALLS AND RIDGES we passed now were brimming with color. Autumn had descended on the canyons even as we left the last plateaus behind. Spruce, pine, and cottonwood trees covered every ridgeline, and red and yellow leaves weighted down the white aspen and left a carpet of color wherever they had fallen. Shadows came early to the canyons, though, and with them the cool, crisp air of fall.

It was nearly October now. We had made good time under Spenser's leadership, even with the various delays. The upward trail was rugged, and it meandered through several deep inclines, where rocks and sagebrush scattered the slopes and creek beds offered little water this time of year. The route presented one more significant challenge, the wagon master told us, speaking again of the descent into the Valley. Toe promised to stay on until that job was done, seeing the labor it entailed, and Spenser was glad to have the extra muscle.

We had passed through Cave Creek Draw, as Spenser called it, and into Echo and East Canyons and other unnamed gorges where mountains towered on either side of us and where the trail was worn with the tracks of a thousand wagons and the footprints of countless souls who had walked this route over the last twenty years. Spenser pointed out Big Mountain looming before us with its 4,700-foot crest, which we would climb. "From there you'll see the Valley," he said, "spread out before us like the Lord's own Eden, and you'll know it's been worth the struggle."

I thought of Leah and how the moment would be for her after all she'd suffered. I was glad Toe and I had brought her here and been baptized and joined this bunch of woebegone Norwegians and stiff-collared Englishmen. Their faith had strengthened me. I was proud of making the journey as well as finding the destination. Still, Leah and I hadn't spoken for several days, and I couldn't shed the bitterness I felt.

Some teamsters from the west joined us as we were getting set to traverse the last sharp decline before winding our way up Big Mountain. The men were burly guides from Salt Lake assigned to meet the trains and help them chain up for the worst part of the descent. One was Brother Wallace, and the other called himself Blue Yodel. They welcomed Spenser and the rest of us with wide smiles and noisy adulation.

"We seen your train three days ago from way up top," said Wallace. "There's two or three outfits behind yours, and we'll get them all in by mid-October. Got to beat the snow, as usual."

Spenser knew Blue Yodel and shook his beefy hand with vigor. "You got an ugly mug, Blue," he said, "but there's no face I'm happier to see!" Spenser introduced us all around. Wallace and Blue Yodel generally met the wagons for the descent of Big Mountain. But they'd been cutting some extra logs in the canyon east of there, they said, and decided to lend a hand as we dipped into the bottom. The wood was cut evenly and stacked on sledges the men had hauled out with their teams, and they immediately set to work chaining the thick logs to the wagon axles. Toe and I jumped in to help and were soon lying on our backs, wrapping a tight chain around the undercarriages at Wallace's direction.

Because each wagon was hard to pull on even ground once the logs had been attached, the teams were set on a slight decline while the chains were wrapped and the oxen held tightly until we'd cleared away. Then the teamster hit the first ox with a prod, and gravity did its work, helping the animals move the load while the logs became a necessary brake to prevent disaster.

At a wide space just above a gentle slope, Spenser directed each team and wagon to "steady up," and in short order the first and second outfits were crawling down the hill. Wallace and Blue Yodel wrestled the logs behind each wagon as the oxen were driven into place. There were shouts and orders and not a little cheering as each outfit topped the slope with its bulky, sputtering animals and creaking wheels. Wallace and Yodel knew their business, and the work went well until a small misstep that changed everything.

People milled about as the logs were being chained. Some of the men held on to the animals. Others watched with interest as Yodel spiked the logs and looped the chains around them. Families from the back wagons waited to the side for their turn. Children eagerly watched, running back and forth and shouting when each pair of oxen were at last let go to lumber away with the added weight behind them. The air rang with sharp excitement and even what I guessed to be a little Scandinavian cursing, although most of the Norwegians stayed a ways back on the trail.

Toe and I had crawled under the next wagon to go, lying on our backs beside opposite rear wheels as we looped the chains around the axles. Suddenly, Toe chuckled when he saw a familiar face kneeling down and grinning at him through the big spokes of the wheel, which lurched occasionally as the wagon shifted. It was Gracie, framed by the spokes and laughing at Toe's unlikely position and the axle grease that was dripping in his eye.

"Toe!" she giggled, leaning in. "I see you through the bars!" Fearlessly, she tried sliding her little body between the spokes and frowned with impertinence when he playfully told her to move back.

"You stay off that wheel now," he called out, busy with the chain. "You'll get stuck between them spokes, and then what would we do?"

"I won't get stuck," said Gracie. "There's lots of room, and I like the way it rocks now and then."

"All the same," continued Toe, "you best stay off that wheel. Sometimes it rocks too much."

Obediently, Grace slid back from the spokes and watched awhile, still fascinated by whatever Toe was doing. Suddenly she crawled to the front of the wheel, apparently hoping to squirm beneath the wagon.

Whether it was the outside ox that restlessly jerked the yoke or a log that suddenly lost its chain, at that moment the heavy wagon lurched and rolled, whipping my end sideways and snapping the wheel beside me off its axle. The box dropped down but not enough to do me any harm. It was the screams I heard on Toe's side that set my heart to racing.

"She's run over!" a woman shouted. "The wheel got her right across the middle. Oh, Lawdy! Lawdy! That poor child!"

It took a few seconds to pull myself from underneath the wagon, and in that time an alarm had traveled up the trail, repeated by every horrified tongue. *The front wagon slipped on its axles and crushed a little girl!*

I heard a ghastly moan and then a shriek that rose above the other voices in agony. Leah emerged in terror from the crowd and flew toward the disabled wagon before anyone could stop her.

"Gracie! Gracieeee!" She fell to her knees beside the wheel and then rose up again, clasping her hands to her head as she frantically whirled about. "No, no, no!"

Joseph Spenser was the first to grab Leah and hold on. Wrapping his arms around her, he pulled her away from the wagon as she began to fight and pound him with her fists and plead with him to let her get to Grace.

"There now. It's best you don't go any closer," he tried to tell her.

"She's under there!" screamed Leah. "It's my baby! It's my baby! We've got to help her!"

With the crowd circling behind me, women sobbing and stunned men looking on, I crawled on my belly past the wheel rim and gazed into the space beneath the wagon. The sight I beheld will remain with me forever, for there was Toe covered in dust and grease and cobwebs from his head to his hands and hanging onto Gracie for dear life.

"I yanked her in," he whispered hoarsely, "just before that big wheel bolted, just in time."

Gracie was staring in wide-eyed shock as I moved closer, and it was only when I reached to touch her that she trembled and began to cry. "Are you all right, darlin'? Do you hurt anywhere?"

"I'm all right with Toe," said Gracie, whimpering. "But I'm scared to let go of him."

Wallace and Yodel were reaching for me as I pulled myself out, still belly down but shouting at the top of my lungs, "She's alive! She's all right! Not a scratch!"

Grace came next, pushed into the light by Toe, who had never looked so filthy. Shaken almost to helplessness, Leah looked at Grace as if she were a ghost and dropped to her knees, gripping Spenser's arm to break the fall. Her hands flew to her mouth as Gracie ran to her.

She was still sobbing uncontrollably several seconds later while the child continued to cling tightly to her neck. "My Gracie! Oh, my Gracie!" she kept repeating hysterically.

Suddenly, as if moved by an unseen power, Joseph Spenser knelt down next to Leah. Whispering gently, he placed his big hand on her shoulder and left it there until her panic eased. Then he drew a small tincture bottle from his coat and poured a few drops of oil in her hair. Laying his hands upon her head, he spoke with the voice of an angel, and all of us who stood nearby were changed forever by his prayer.

"O, God, our Father, by the power of the priesthood which I hold, I bless this dear young woman to be whole again. For too long she has suffered for the sins of others. For too long she has carried the terrible burden of regret and self-recrimination. For too long the sins of Lawrence have plagued her and the real Zion has been out of reach. Give this woman back her sense of worth. Give her back the things she lost. Let this rescue of her little daughter be a sign from thee, dear Lord, of how much Leah Donaldson is loved."

Leah's breathless sobbing ceased. A familiar radiance covered her face, and her eyes were full of light again. As she held Grace up to look at her, I envisioned Addie there, charmed by Leah's smile. She squeezed Grace all the tighter while Spenser helped her to her feet.

The three of them embraced, and she thanked him. A cheer went up from the people circled round, and I couldn't help but join in the jubilation. Grace's rescue, Spenser's prayer—both had moved me even as I accepted that Leah's Zion would be different from my own.

"How did Spenser know to pray like that?" asked Toe in the evening after things had settled down. "He had no firsthand view of Leah's troubles, and yet he seemed to know the burdens of her heart. I've never witnessed such a power, Ethan. I swear, I never have."

★

She came to us later, after the camp had settled at the bottom of the slope, after the excitement of the afternoon had ended and Gracie had been comfortably put to bed. It was very dark, but Leah knew that Toe and I would still be up, stirring the last coals in our fire pit, picking out the stars we knew, remembering our youthful days in Lawrence.

We jumped up when she appeared, and I had to swallow hard. She looked so beautiful in the reflection of the lantern that she carried. "How can I ever thank you, Toe?" She spoke softly, placed her head against his chest, and clung to him as he ran his fingers through her hair. She had never called him Toe until this moment.

"That little gal means a lot to me, Miss Leah. I wasn't gonna see her hurt."

I stepped closer, and Leah's arms encircled us both. "I love you, boys," she said. "I wish Bobbie and Addie were here and time could take us back again to that last summer in Lawrence. Remember how we sat there on the porch and you all told me about your spying on me and Joby Crockett? It seems like centuries ago. Bobbie was a firecracker." She smiled. "I miss him so."

"Bobbie's always here in spirit," said Toe. "He's with me all the time. As for Addie, she's most growed up, but we got Gracie to remind us what little girls are like!"

"Yes, we do!" said Leah, affirmatively.

Toe slid his fingers down Leah's arm, taking her hand and finally letting go when he'd touched her fingers. "Good night, Miss Leah." He moved away from us into the shadows as if he knew his cue.

For the first time in many days, Leah and I stood alone together.

"I'm sure glad Gracie's all right," I said, looking at her tentatively, "and you too. Even when she came out from underneath that wagon, I thought you never would stop shaking."

"I haven't been so scared since Lawrence, with you and Addie in the priest hole and Lonnie Hodge ready to burn the house. I loved you then, Ethan, as I love Gracie now. For me, you'll always be that boy I loved, not the man you've become."

"I learned today I'm not quite a man as yet, at least not the man that you deserve." I hesitated, trying to find the words. Maybe I was just seeing a way to save face since Leah had rejected me. Maybe I'd have still pleaded for her if she'd given me half a chance. But that prayer of Spenser's blessed me too, I think. Its power opened my eyes to reality and steeled me for it. "It took a seasoned elder of the Church to pray for you and save your life," I said to Leah. "I'm just a kid when it comes to stuff like that. Joesph Spenser called down the power of the Lord, and he knew how to do it. I'm not that kind of man yet. I've got a lot to learn."

She put her arms around me, nestling her head against my heart. I held her close and felt as warm and loved as I ever wanted to be. "Will you be all right?" she said. "Will you be all right without me?"

Stung by the lesson of the bitter choice, I nodded and waited for her to lift her eyes to mine. In my coat pocket was the ivory pendant I'd taken back from Lonnie Hodge after he'd stolen it from Leah's room, my mother's ivory pendant with the golden chain. "I want you to have this," I whispered. "I gave it to you years ago, and it's still yours."

"Oh, Ethan." She put it on and let me help her with the clasp. "I'll treasure it," she said, toying with the oval in her fingers.

"What about you?" I asked her.

"What do you mean, what about me?"

"You asked if I'd be all right, and I want to ask the same."

She hesitated, and her eyes brightened as they never had in weeks.

"Well, what about you?" I asked her again, and she was suddenly luminous, laughing joyously.

"Oh, Ethan, don't you know? We're here! Zion's over that next mountain, and you're going to stand with me tomorrow as we look down on it—my dream come true, the promised valley, the City on a Hill!"

★

Our line of wagons struggled up the incline the next morning, clinging to the edge of Big Mountain as we followed the trail. At the crest, the sky was crisp and clear, and we looked out with wonder at the panorama which spread before us, our first glimpse of the long valley—its hay and wheat and corn ready to be harvested, its little villages in the south clustered about with trees, its benches and foothills descending at our feet, and its desert lake shimmering in the distance like a mirror in the sand.

The city itself, nestled at the head of the spreading plain, was small by Eastern standards. Its balanced grid of streets and avenues hardly extended past the flatlands on the valley floor. Still, trees and orchards and churches were evident from our vantage point, and the chimneys were somehow welcoming, telling us that all over town a hearty breakfast was being served. The Saints had been in the Valley twenty-one years by the time I saw it, and in the wilderness they had truly built their Zion.

It was the climax of our journey. The day would be spent chaining up again for the difficult descent into the final canyon and over the benches above the town. Toe and I would help with that task. Then we'd spend a few nights in the city, resting our horses, looking the place over, and maybe even meeting Brigham Young. Spenser told us, laughingly, that he had "connections" at the top. So I guessed it might be possible.

I watched as the folks from our company gathered at the crest to finally see their Zion. There was a lot of cheering. Some of the men waved their hats and propped their children on their shoulders for a better view. Many of the women cried and laughed at the same time. The Norwegians were the funniest to see, garbling excitedly in that strange language of theirs with lots of happy nods and *ja, ja, ja* and not a word of English. They'd come the farthest, I suppose, and deserved to celebrate the moment in their own way.

Joseph Spenser, waving his hat with everybody else, made a point to shake hands with Toe and me, knowing we were headed back to Lawrence the first chance we got. "I'm more than grateful you boys came along," he said, "and I hope you feel the same."

Leah and Grace were a few yards off, viewing Zion from the best vantage point and conversing happily with the Meltons and others.

Spenser nodded in Leah's direction. "You needn't worry," he said quietly. "Zion'll take good care of her. I'll see to it."

I believed him. Since the blessing by the wagon, I knew Leah would be all right, and I could go home without her, finding my own Zion in the ashes of my shattered town, where I was needed most. Leah had given me that perspective. *Zion is an idea as well as a place*, she used to say, and now I knew the meaning of those words. And I knew that if I carried Zion in my heart, Leah would always be there too, pushing me toward a good life because of all she'd done for me.

As people began to disperse and return to their wagons, several of them lingered, reluctant to turn away from the majestic view they'd struggled so long to see. Among them I noticed Leah with Gracie at her side. They faced away from me, toward the Valley, perhaps envisioning their future on that broad plain. Leah's long, dark hair, tossed a little by the breeze, fell to her waist, and when she turned in profile, I saw a single braid plaited with ribbons, drawn back above her ear. It reminded me of the Leah I first knew, a pretty girl on Amos Willard's arm.

As I paused a moment watching, Joseph Spenser approached Leah and stood with her and Gracie gazing over Zion. They looked like they belonged together, a strong and faithful man, a little child, and my Leah. I wondered if Spenser appreciated what he had—besides the promised fertile plain of Zion spreading out before him. I guessed he did, for I saw him place a gentle hand on Leah's shoulder before I finally turned away.

Afterword

WHILE THE STORY OF LEAH Donaldson and Ethan Pace is fiction, this novel's centerpiece event, the massacre at Lawrence, Kansas, in 1863, is historically accurate. The Southern raider William Clarke Quantrill led a column of several hundred guerrillas into the town on the morning of August 21 and proceeded to pillage and destroy, murdering more than 150 men and boys and burning many of the homes and businesses. Prominent men were targeted, and several died while their frantic wives pleaded with the killers to spare them. The murder of Judge Louis Carpenter, as described in the novel, was particularly brutal, as his young wife, Mary, would later testify.

Mayor George Collamore suffocated in the well where he was hiding, and a friend who tried to rescue him was also killed. Many innocent civilians met their deaths in the cornfields surrounding Lawrence, run down by men on horses as they attempted to escape. Reverend S. S. Snyder of the United Brethren Church was the first to die that morning, shot down near his home as he milked his cow. The youngest victim of the massacre was fourteen-year-old Bobbie Martin, who was wearing a blue uniform his mother had made for him. I have fictionalized this boy as a character in the novel and tried to make his death as significant in the story as it surely was in reality.

The great newspaper editor William Allen White once called the cemetery in Lawrence "the Arlington of Kansas." As stories of the massacre are repeated in fiction and in history, these little-known victims of the Civil War are hopefully acknowledged and remembered.

About the Author

AN AWARD-WINNING PUBLIC SCHOOL TEACHER for nearly thirty years in Southern Idaho, Lynne Larson has written numerous articles, essays, and short stories for both regional and national publications. Since her retirement from the classroom, she has continued to promote education, particularly in history and literature, and is a frequent speaker for book clubs and service groups. She has published six novels, all of which generally reflect her love of Western lore and Americana. A graduate of Brigham Young University, Mrs. Larson also holds an MA in English from Idaho State University. She and her husband, Kent, currently live in American Fork, Utah. They are the parents of three grown children.